Also by
CHRISTOPHER EDGE

The Many Worlds of Albie Bright

The Jamie Drake Equation

The Infinite Lives of Maisie Day

The Longest Night of Charlie Noon

The Twelve Minutes to Midnight trilogy:

Twelve Minutes to Midnight

Shadows of the Silver Screen

The Black Crow Conspiracy

Praise for
CHRISTOPHER EDGE

"No ordinary author. His stories fizz with ideas,
the perfect fodder for the child with more
questions than answers."
The Times, Children's Book of the Week

"A writer of genuine originality ... Edge creates strong
characters who come alive on the page and he has
a thriller writer's feel for suspense."
The Guardian

"A heart-stopping adventure with thrills and twists."
The Sunday Times

"Quite extraordinary."
The Spectator

"This is the best read I've had in ages.
Give it to any child you come across."
Lucy Mangan

"No one writes books like Christopher Edge."
Kiran Millwood Hargrave

"This book is out-of-this-world,
edge-of-your-seat AMAZING!"
Lauren St John

"Eye-poppingly original.
Grabs hold of your brain – then tugs at your heart."
Jonathan Stroud

ESCAPE ROOM

CHRISTOPHER EDGE

nosy
crow

First published in the UK in 2022 by Nosy Crow Ltd
Wheat Wharf, 27a Shad Thames,
London, SE1 2XZ, UK

Nosy Crow Eireann Ltd
44 Orchard Grove, Kenmare,
Co Kerry, V93 FY22, Ireland

Nosy Crow and associated logos are trademarks and/or registered
trademarks of Nosy Crow Ltd

14

The lines of poetry found in chapter 10 are taken from "There is
another sky" from *Poems by Emily Dickinson, First Series*

A CIP catalogue record for this book is available from
the British Library.

Printed and bound in the UK by Clays Ltd, Elcograf S.p.A
Typeset by Tiger Media

Papers used by Nosy Crow are made from wood grown in
sustainable forests

ISBN: 978 1 78800 796 2

www.nosycrow.com
www.christopheredge.co.uk

For Alex and Josie

1

This is The Escape.

It looks just how I imagined it would look: a neon blade of a building rising above the dark windowless warehouses that surround it. LED lights shimmer across its mirrored surfaces as I approach, catching my reflection in a kaleidoscope of colour.

I'm buzzing with excitement. This is my reward for working so hard: an evening of adventure at The Escape.

That's if I can find my way in.

I'm not sure at first if this is part of the game. I skirt round the edge of the building, searching for the entrance, but all I can see is an endless wall of glass. It's as though whoever designed this building forgot to put in a front door, which is a bit of a problem if you want to pay them a visit. Maybe that's why they called it The Escape – because it's so hard to find the way out.

Then I spot it. Halfway along the wall, what I thought was a reflection is actually a revolving door, the sleek panels that are wrapped round the rest of the building bulging gently outwards in a smooth curve of glass. I come to a halt in front of this door, my mirror image reflected in stereo. Stepping forward, I push against the right-hand panel, eager to get the game started at last.

It doesn't move. The door's locked.

Looking up, I see the black ball of a camera lens staring down from the ceiling, a red dot at its centre. Someone's watching me.

I give a friendly wave to the camera.

"It's me – Ami Oswald," I say with a hopeful smile on my face. "I'm here to play."

There's a moment of silence as I wait for an answer. Then the revolving door clicks as the lock is released. This first test passed, I push against the panel again and, as the door swings, I step inside

The Escape.

The air feels instantly cooler, the low humming sound of the traffic outside replaced by a hushed silence as the revolving door closes behind me. I'm in some kind of lobby, a large circular space that looks like the bridge of a spaceship. The curved walls ripple with the same soothing patterns of colour that shimmered across the outside, while the lobby is lit by concentric circles of lights that shine down from the ceiling. There's a round reception desk in the middle of this space, its surface gleaming with the same bright whiteness that covers the floor. It looks like you could fit a thousand people in here, but, as I look around, there's only me.

I step towards the reception desk, hearing the sharp rap of my footsteps echoing back across the empty lobby. I thought there'd be somebody here to greet me, but as I reach the desk, the only thing I can see is a name badge left waiting for me.

AMI

Picking it up, I pin the badge to my top. At least they've spelled my name right – Ami with an "i" not a "y".

When he made the booking, Dad said that this

place was home to the ultimate escape room. Some people call them escape games or locked-room adventures, but the way they work is always the same. A team of players is locked in a room together to solve the clues and puzzles they find before time runs out. I like solving puzzles, so Dad reckoned a trip here would be the perfect gift for me. But it looks like I'll be playing alone.

"Hello."

The greeting makes me jump halfway out of my skin.

I turn to see a girl standing right beside me. Her eyes are hidden behind shocking pink sunglasses, but the smile on her face beams even more brightly than they do. Dark braids fall loosely round her shoulders, a handful of freckles dotted across her dark brown skin. She's wearing a cap-sleeved T-shirt with a vintage games console on the front, black-and-white checked trousers and neon-green trainers. This girl looks seriously cool.

"Do you work here?" I ask.

Removing her sunglasses, the girl shakes her head and points to the name badge on her T-shirt.

"I'm Adjoa," she says with a smile. "I'm here to play the game – just like you."

I smile back at Adjoa; her enthusiasm is infectious. Inside, I feel the same surge of excitement that I felt when I first laid eyes on The Escape. Maybe this is going to be fun after all.

"So where are the others?" Adjoa asks, raising a quizzical eyebrow. "I thought we were meant to be a team."

As if in reply, we hear the whirr of the revolving door and turn to see two boys entering the lobby. They look about the same age as me – the same age as Adjoa too now she's taken off her sunglasses – but apart from that I can't help noticing how different they seem.

The first boy moves quickly, his short blond hair turning ash-white beneath the lights as he strides purposefully towards us. His restless eyes dart from side to side.

"So this is the place?" he asks, his voice echoing across the cavernous space. "Doesn't look like much to me."

With his black zip top and running trousers, he looks like he's heading for the gym, although this is probably a wise choice of outfit. As well as solving puzzles and clues, escape rooms can sometimes make you sweat a bit too, with physical challenges to beat. You might find yourself dodging past tripwire traps or crawling through a laser maze. It all depends on the theme of the game you play.

Across the lobby, the second boy is still standing just inside the door, looking around in wide-eyed wonder. With his baggy grey jumper and khaki cords, *he* doesn't look ready for any kind of physical challenge. Not unless we're going to be escaping from the fashion police. But my eyes are drawn to the Rubik's cube that he's holding, his long fingers absent-mindedly twisting its squares. Intrigued, I watch as the colourful patterns flickering across the faces of the cube echo those still shimmering across the walls.

The first boy swaggers to a halt at the desk.

"Hi," I start to say, but the boy just ignores me, reaching across to pick up two more badges that I hadn't noticed before. Pinning one that says OSCAR to his zip top, he looks back over his shoulder.

"Hey!" he calls out to the boy still dawdling at the door. "Are you Ibrahim?"

Glancing across at the sound of Oscar's shout, the second boy nods. His dark scraggly hair is swept back from his face and his angular features shift into a pensive frown. "That's me."

Ibrahim hurries to join us, the cube still click-clacking in his hands. Oscar holds out the badge with IBRAHIM printed across the front.

"Thanks," Ibrahim says as he sets his Rubik's cube down on the reception desk, the puzzle now solved with each face showing a single colour. Taking his name badge, he smiles shyly at the rest of us. "Are you all here for the game too?"

"Welcome to the team!" Adjoa says brightly, turning the full beam of her smile in Ibrahim's direction. "Do you think we should call ourselves the Awesome Foursome or maybe the Fantastic Four? We need to pick a name that'll look good on top of the leader board."

"We don't need a stupid team name to win this game," Oscar sneers, but then a new voice chips in with a suggestion.

"How about the Five Mind?"

Turning round in surprise, I see a girl standing on the other side of the reception desk. She doesn't look much older than me – twelve or thirteen maybe. Her straight black hair is cut into a sharp bob, dark eyes shining from beneath her fringe. It takes me a moment to work out what she's called as her name badge is lost among all the others covering her denim jacket. Then I spot it, nestled next to the smiley faces, superhero symbols and CND signs.

MIN

"I mean, if this game really is as tough as people say it is," the girl continues, "we're going to have to put our heads together to win."

There's a silent pause as we all try to work out where she's come from. Shifting patterns of colour flicker across the curved walls. The only door into this place is the one we all walked through and I didn't see Min come in.

"I like it," Adjoa says, breaking the silence. "It's a pun, isn't it? Like a hive mind where people share their intelligence? There are five of us and if we all work together then we'll be five times as smart."

Min nods her head. "Maybe even smarter," she says. "What do you think, Ami?"

I glance around the lobby, wanting to make sure that nobody else is hiding out of sight. There are no more name badges waiting to be collected. Standing beneath the bright lights, Adjoa, Oscar, Ibrahim and Min stare back at me. It looks like this is my team.

"Sounds good to me," I agree. "But when's the game going to start?"

And then the lights go out and the shimmering colours that encircle the walls dissolve in a burst of static. For a second I feel a flicker of fear but then this is swept away by an onrushing excitement as the face of a man appears there instead.

It's starting.

Game on.

2

"Welcome to The Escape," the man says, his voice filling the space. "I am the Host and you have been chosen to save the world."

He looks like the kind of man you always see reading the news on TV, neatly trimmed with his features in perfect proportion. The walls of the lobby have been transformed into a wrap-around media screen and the Host is staring out from every surface. His short dark hair is flecked with grey and the lines on his face crease in a concerned expression.

"You are humanity's last hope," he

continues. "I can only pray that you will succeed where we have failed."

He's making it sound like the end of the world, but I can't stop myself from smiling. This is how these escape games always begin – the game master setting up the story and explaining what you need to do to win. This might be breaking into a bank vault to steal a priceless treasure or searching a scientific laboratory to discover a secret formula. Every escape room has its own unique mission. And now he's going to tell us what *we* need to do to save the world…

I glance around at the others, their faces lit by the light from the screen. Ibrahim peers intently at the Host, his head tilted slightly to one side, while next to him Oscar stands with his arms folded across his chest. Catching my gaze, Adjoa flashes me an excited smile and then nods in Min's direction. I look across to see that Min's pulled out a notebook from somewhere and is scribbling furiously as the Host continues to speak.

"We need you to find the Answer."

I can hear the capital letter in his voice as a news ticker starts to scroll across the bottom of the screen.

Find the Answer. Save the world. Find the Answer.

Save the world. Find the Answer. Save the world. Find the Answer.

"All you need to succeed is hidden inside The Escape. The puzzles that you find and the challenges you face might seem impossible at first, but for you nothing is impossible. Look around carefully. Everything is part of the game. Use your mind to find the Answer. It's what we need to save the world."

Min looks up from her notebook. "If you want us to find the Answer," she says, "don't you need to tell us what the question is?"

I thought this was a pre-recorded video, but the Host pauses, his gaze turning in Min's direction.

"We have so many questions," he replies, shaking his head sadly. "And there are more asked of us each day. Burning questions, billion-dollar questions, but it's all now just a question of time. The clock is ticking – the countdown has begun."

Staring out from the screen, the Host's flint-grey eyes seem to fix on to mine.

"Find the Answer," he says. "Find the Answer before it's too late."

I don't know what he means. He's talking in riddles, but I'm supposed to be good at solving those. Before I can get my brain into gear, I hear Oscar pipe up.

"Find the Answer, save the world, bada bing bada boom." He snaps his fingers with a click that echoes around the room. "So what are we waiting for?"

There's a grinding metallic sound and the face of the Host starts to split into two. I hear Adjoa gasp in surprise as the screens that circle the walls slide apart to reveal an open door. This must be the way in to the first of the escape rooms – the place where this game really begins.

Beyond the door, the room is in total darkness, but Oscar is already striding into it. The curved walls of the lobby now shimmer with colour again, the scrolling shapes of arrows showing which way to go.

"I will be monitoring your every move," the Host says, his disembodied voice floating free as Ibrahim, Adjoa and Min quickly follow in Oscar's footsteps. "The path you take through The Escape will lead you closer to me. Take nothing for granted. Question everything. The Answer might be found in the most unexpected of places."

I hurry to catch up with the others, heading for

the darkness of the room.

It's time to save the world.

3

I take a deep breath, straining my eyes against the absolute blackness that surrounds me. I can hear noises in the darkness: the creak of floorboards and then a heavy thud that sounds like a door slamming shut.

I've never been afraid of the dark, but it's still kind of a relief when a light finally flickers into life, filling the space with a warm yellow glow.

We're standing in what looks like an attic. A bare bulb hangs from the ceiling, illuminating a sloping roof and white-plaster walls that are criss-crossed with cobwebs. And between these walls piles of electronic equipment are stacked everywhere that I look: ancient computer systems, keyboards, monitors and hard-drive towers. A trail of rainbow ribbon cables snake from the innards of a black bin bag, while another looks like it's filled with CDs and DVDs, the silver discs spilling out across the floor. There are cardboard boxes and old packing cases everywhere, all filled with even more tech.

Everything is covered in a thick layer of dust. This looks like the place old computers come to die.

Adjoa and Oscar are already rummaging among the piles, Oscar pressing buttons on everything that he finds.

"This stuff is seriously old-school," Adjoa says, crouching down as she reads out the names etched on the plastic casing. "*Altair 8800, Acorn Atom, Commodore 64*. These aren't computers. They're antiques."

"That's why nothing works," Oscar growls, flicking a switch on a chunky monitor from off to on. Its box-like screen stays blank. "It's just electronic junk."

Glancing around, I try to find the door where we came in. There's no sign of it underneath the eaves behind us – only a bare brick wall. Turning back, I peer beyond the mounds of electronics into the gloom at the far end of the attic, but all I can see there is the shape of an old armchair, its back turned towards me. There's no door there either. And anyway, that wasn't the way we came in.

The only door I *can* see is a trapdoor in the middle of the floor. Ibrahim is already crouching over it, twisting the catch to try to pull it open. He slowly shakes his head. "It's locked."

Standing next to me, Min scribbles in her notebook.

"Only one visible escape route," she mutters. "Locked."

"Don't worry," I say, reaching out a hand to help Ibrahim back to his feet. "That's how these games work. We've got to solve the puzzles to find the way out."

"What puzzles?" Oscar snorts, breaking open a cardboard box and peering inside at the contents before shoving it to one side. "This isn't an escape room – it's more like a jumble sale."

An avalanche of cassette tapes slide out from the tear that Oscar's made in the box, falling to the floor in a clatter of plastic.

"Everything is part of the game," Min says, glancing up from her notebook. "We've just got to work out what we need to do."

I look around the attic again. Beneath the light, the yellowing hard drives and dead computer screens stare back at me like tombstones. I don't want to agree with him, but I can't help feeling that Oscar's right. How are we supposed to work out what we need to do when nothing works?

Ibrahim picks up the end of one of the computer cables. "Maybe we just need to plug this in?"

Oscar fixes him with a withering stare. "Find the plug, save the world," he says, his words dripping with sarcasm. "Yeah, I'm sure that'll work."

Adjoa turns on him angrily. "Well, what's your bright idea?" she asks, jabbing her finger in Oscar's direction. "This stuff's got to be here for a reason. If we can get it to work, then it might give us a clue."

"We need to take this place apart," Oscar replies. "If there are any clues hidden among these piles of junk, then that's the only way we're going to find them."

Adjoa narrows her eyes. "That's the stupidest idea I've ever heard."

"See if you can—"

"Can we just—"

"Give me the—"

Everyone starts talking at once. I stare at them in disbelief, my gaze flicking from Oscar to Adjoa, then to Ibrahim and Min, their voices getting louder and louder as they try to make themselves heard.

This is my team. We're supposed to work together to find the Answer.

We don't stand a chance.

I turn away. Dad said this game was going to be fun, but it's turning into a total headache.

Then, above their arguing voices, I catch a strange noise at the very edge of my hearing. A metallic clicking like a key being turned in a lock.

I glance down at the trapdoor, but the sound isn't coming from there.

"Hey," I say, trying to get everyone's attention. "Can you hear that?"

Nobody's listening, except to their own voices.

The clicking noise comes again and I look around, trying to work out exactly where it's coming from.

At first I think it might be one of the computers but as I trace a path through the piles of out-of-date hardware, I realise that the sound is coming from the far end of the attic. I peer into the gloom, unable to see anything beyond the high back of the broad armchair.

I push on. Tiny specks of dust dance before my eyes and the shadows lengthen around me now as I block out the light. The sound is getting louder too, like metallic teeth catching on a spinning wheel. I shiver, the arguing voices behind me fading as I focus all my attention on finding out what is making this noise.

And then I see him: the man sitting motionless in the armchair. No, not exactly motionless. The white-gloved fingers of his right hand drum against the desk that he's seated behind, the rhythmic clicks worming their way inside my mind. In the centre of the desk a chessboard is set up for a game. My heart skips a beat as I glance up to meet the man's gaze, his dark-grey eyes staring into mine. He looks like the kind of magician you'd find in a book of old fairy tales. His beard is black and pointed, a severe expression set upon his face. He's dressed in fire-red robes, the collar and sleeves trimmed with fur, while his dark features glower beneath a bejewelled turban.

My eyes are drawn to this precious stone. It looks

like a black pearl pinned to the front of his turban, a red dot gleaming in the centre. I remember the camera lens I saw outside The Escape and hear an echo of the Host's words inside my mind. *I will be monitoring your every move.*

He's watching me now.

The man's fingers stop their drumming, and the silence that follows is even worse.

"Ami!" Adjoa calls out from the other side of the attic. "What've you found?"

"I think you need to see this," I say, keeping my eyes fixed on the camera lens. "All of you."

4

There's a scramble as the others rush to join me, all arguments forgotten as they crowd round the desk.

"What is this?" Oscar asks. He raps his knuckles on the table. "Hello? Is anybody home?"

The man doesn't move, his expression unchanged as he stares blankly ahead.

"It's the Chess-Player of Maelzel," Min says, her dark eyes sparkling with delight. "An automaton that was built over 250 years ago."

As soon as she says this, I breathe a sigh of relief. I didn't know at first if this man was real or not. Some of these escape rooms use actors to make the game seem more believable, but as I look more closely I can now see the sheen of his waxwork skin.

"You mean like a robot?" Adjoa asks.

"Kind of," Min replies. "An automaton was a machine that could imitate the actions of a living creature. There were mechanical birds and clockwork dancers – these early robots performed the same repetitive movements every time they were switched on – but the Chess-Player of Maelzel was different. Its inventor claimed that his machine could defeat any human player at the game of chess."

With a clicking whirr the man slowly moves his head from side to side, his deep-set eyes surveying the chessboard in front of him. I hold my breath, waiting to see what he does next. His left arm jerks forward, the movement so sudden that I take a step back in surprise. Fingers splayed, his hand descends to pick up a white pawn directly in front of his king, moving the piece two squares forward before setting the pawn down again. As his arm jerkily returns to its original position, I realise what we're supposed to do.

We've got to play.

Leaning forward, I quickly slide a black pawn forward one square.

"Hey," Oscar says, raising his voice in protest. "Who said you could play the robot?"

I shoot him a look. "I'm a chess champion," I say, pointing to a pin on my top. On the front of this badge a gold knight stands proudly beneath the word GRANDMASTER. "Do you want to win this game or not?"

That shuts him up.

It was Dad who taught me chess. We used to play endless games that sometimes went on for days. The thing I like about it is that you have to follow the rules. Each player begins with the same sixteen pieces: eight pawns, two rooks, two knights, two bishops, one queen and one king. And the aim of the game is always the same – to attack your opponent's king until it can't escape. Checkmate.

But to get there you've got to be clever, working out the best way to attack your opponent's pieces while defending your own. It's a game that needs logic, strategy and skill, and I'm pretty good at those things. That's why Dad stopped playing me in the end – I kept winning all the time.

The chess player whirrs into life once more, his

left arm reaching out to pick up another pawn. As the sound of clockwork gears click into position, he sets this pawn down alongside the first – a front line of soldiers advancing towards my army of black chess pieces. But before his arm even returns to its resting position, I slide another of my pawns forward to face his.

The clockwork man pauses for a moment, fingers trembling as his hand hovers above the board. I don't think he was expecting me to move so fast. His head slowly moves from side to side again. It looks like he's thinking, but I think this is just for show. Then his arm jerks back as he picks up a knight and moves it into play.

That's what I thought he was going to do.

I take his pawn.

First blood to me.

"Nice move," Adjoa says as I place the captured pawn on the table. I smile, but before I can start to feel too pleased with myself, the automaton strikes back.

With a clicking whirr I watch his gloved hand pick up the same knight again, this time transporting it sideways to capture my pawn.

"Yeah," Oscar says, patting me on the back as the

man places my chess piece on his side of the desk. "Nice move, champ."

I ignore him, focusing on the board in front of me.

When you're playing chess, you need to look ahead: working out the moves you can make to improve your position. There are sixty-four squares on the board, but these give you so many possibilities. What I've got to do now is choose the right one.

Reaching out, I move one of my knights forward, but as his machinery whirrs the man does the same, so I move my other knight too.

"I don't know if this is what we're supposed to be doing," Min says, her voice urgent in my ear.

"What do you mean?" I ask, trying not to let myself get distracted as the clockwork man slides his bishop into play.

"The Chess-Player of Maelzel was a fake," Min replies. "It wasn't a real machine. Whenever it played chess, there was someone hiding behind the scenes making the moves."

"You mean like *The Wizard of Oz*?" Adjoa asks. "I love that film." She clicks the heels of her neon-green trainers together. "*There's no place like home.*"

Keeping my eyes fixed to the chessboard, I move the pawn in front of my king forward one square. It's all going to plan, my strategy taking shape inside my mind.

"That's right," Min says as the chess player moves his second knight into play. "And it's only when Dorothy unmasks the real wizard that she's able to find her way home. Maybe that's what we need to do to find the Answer. We need to unmask the person who's controlling this machine."

I'm only half listening, keeping my attention trained on the game. I can see the moves I need to make unfolding one after another. I move my pawn to attack his first knight.

The chess player whirrs into life again, his left hand reaching out to pick up his knight. As the clockwork gears click, he moves this at a right angle to capture another of my pawns.

"He's winning," Oscar says.

I shake my head as I move my queen into play. "I don't think so."

Beneath his turban, the chess player rolls his lifeless eyes. If someone is controlling him like a puppet, it looks like they don't know what to do next.

His left arm slowly jerks across the board, first moving his king and then a rook as he castles these pieces. A defensive move, but he can't defend everything.

Smiling, I move one of my pawns forward, taking his knight.

Advantage me.

I look around, waiting for the congratulations, but the others seem more interested in what Min's doing as she crouches at the front of the desk.

"The operator was usually hidden inside," she says, inspecting the doors and drawers there that hide its interior from view. "We just need to get these open somehow."

"I found this," Ibrahim says, holding up a small silver key. "It didn't fit the lock on the trapdoor, but maybe it'll work here."

There's a metallic clicking as the chess player slowly shakes his head, as if he's warning us about what we're about to do next.

Min tries the key in the lock on the front of the desk and I hear the same sound again.

"It works," Min says, glancing up with a grin. "Now let's see who the wizard really is."

We all crowd round as she opens the doors,

revealing what's hidden inside the desk.

There's nothing there. No clockwork cogs and gears, no hidden machinery. No sign of a puppetmaster pulling the chess-player's strings. The space beneath the desk is completely empty. All I can see through a grille at the back are the automaton's fire-red robes.

"I don't understand," Min says.

A whirring noise draws my eyes back to the chess player. His left arm is jerking forward again, fingers closing round his bishop and then moving it diagonally to attack my king. As he sets the piece down, I hear a single word escape from his lips.

"Check."

His voice sounds strangely human as I stare in disbelief at the board. I hadn't seen this coming. I didn't even think I was under attack. Leaning forward, I quickly move my king out of check.

The whirring of machinery starts again and I watch as the man moves his second bishop into play. I gaze up into his eyes, the sheen of his waxwork features glistening in the gloom. Are we really sure he isn't real?

Feeling flustered, I move one of my pawns forward two spaces. You're allowed to do this when it's the first move your pawn makes, although Dad sometimes forgets this and accuses me of cheating.

The automaton moves his pawn too, putting me under attack.

Everyone's talking at once – offering me advice, suggesting tactics – but I just need to think.

I move my bishop diagonally one square, playing for time.

The clockwork clicking starts again, but I know there's no machinery to make this noise. It's a fake – just like Min said it was – a trick to distract us. The chess-player's arm slowly jerks across the board, moving his rook one square to the left. But maybe the trick was to make us *think* it's not real?

There's no wizard to unmask; only a machine to beat. And that means I've got to win.

I move my knight to attack his bishop and then watch as he moves it back out of range. I move my king. He takes my pawn, so I take his in return. Everyone's silent as they watch the game unfold, the chess pieces dancing around the board: queen, bishop, bishop, rook. And that's when it all goes wrong.

From out of nowhere his rook storms the length of the board, capturing my queen. Stunned, I stare at his gloved hand as it transports my piece to the edge, dropping it with a clunk on his side of the desk.

I'm in deep trouble now.

The queen is the most powerful piece in the game. She can move anywhere on the board, in every direction, any number of squares. If you lose your queen, winning becomes *so* much harder.

With a rush of frustration I move my bishop to take his rook, but this retaliation doesn't make me feel much better. With a clicking whirr another white pawn is pushed forward, the chess player marshalling his pieces in a relentless attack.

I move my own pawns forward, but every move I make just feels like I'm staving off the inevitable. This machine is going to win.

Then Oscar reaches over me. Picking up one of my black knights, he jumps it forward two squares to take the chess-player's queen.

"What are you doing?" I ask as he deposits this stolen piece on my side of the board. "Knights can only move in an L shape – not straight ahead."

"We can cheat," Oscar says, tipping a wink in the direction of my opponent. "Old Clocky here won't know any different."

With a metallic snick, the chess player roughly shakes his head. The white glove of his right hand raps against the desk three times, before he reaches out with his left to replace his white queen back in the position it was stolen from.

"I think he does."

Then the chess player makes his own move, advancing his rook threateningly. I don't know what to do and push my pieces around the board as I react to his probing attacks. It feels like I'm running out of time, his movements sounding like the ticking of a clock. I stare at the pieces that are left on the board, trying to see a way to win.

Near the far corner, one lonely black pawn has almost reached the other side. And, as I look at this piece, I remember. The pawn might be the least powerful piece in the game, but when it reaches the end of the board it can change.

I push the pawn forward one square, then in the same action, reach out to swap it for my queen. With a smile I nod my head towards the opposite corner where the white king is now trapped defenceless.

"Checkmate."

With a clicking whirr the man moves his head from side to side, his dark-grey eyes studying the chessboard in front of him. There's no way out. No move he can make to avoid checkmate. We've won.

He lifts his right arm and, for a second, I think he's going to shake my hand. Then his arm sweeps out in a rage, knocking all the pieces off the board and sending them flying.

Overhead, the lights turn red as a siren begins to blare.

"Ami!" Adjoa calls out. "What's happening?"

I look around the attic, the dead computer screens now blinking into life. Streams of letters and numbers scroll across their displays, the same message repeated again and again.

SELF-DESTRUCT SEQUENCE INITIATED

And then the numbers start to count down.

I turn towards the others, their eyes wide with fear.

"I don't think we were supposed to win."

5

I can't think – my vision is flashing red as the siren blare seems to drown out everything. The others stand there, frozen in shock – all except one.

Ignoring the incessant sound, Min starts to carefully place the scattered chess pieces back in their starting positions, the rows of black and white pawns lining up against each other once more.

"What are you doing?" I ask, my heart hammering in my chest as the bulb overhead pulses with its crimson light.

Picking up a white knight from where

it's fallen, Min leans across the chessboard to return it to its starting square.

"We need to play him again," she says, glancing up to meet the chess-player's dark-eyed gaze. "Let him win and make this stop."

But as this last word escapes Min's lips, she suddenly drops the carved horse with a cry of alarm.

The chessboard is on fire, every chequered square now blazing with a hissing flame. I don't know how this can be happening. There must be burners hidden beneath the desk somewhere and now someone has turned the gas on. Draped over the edge of the board, the chess player's robes ignite and Min recoils as the leaping flames lick at her sleeve. Quickly I drag Min back, beating away the flames as the automaton is set ablaze.

As he burns, I hear a mechanical clicking. The chess player is raising an arm to point his gloved finger directly at me. Through the flames I see his waxen face start to melt, but his dark eyes burn with a triumphant glare.

"Checkmate," he says, his teeth now bared in a rictus grin.

I look around, desperate to find something to put the fire out. Snapping into action, Ibrahim drags a dust sheet off a stack of ancient computer equipment, revealing a row of cracked screens underneath. But as he flings this sheet forward to smother the flames, it just catches fire instead, spreading the blaze across the attic with a whiplash crackle. The scorching heat is so fierce that it forces us back, my eyes flicking between the melting face of the automaton and the message that flashes from every computer screen.

SELF-DESTRUCT SEQUENCE INITIATED
98... 97... 96... 95...

My mind races as I try to work out what's gone wrong. This is The Escape. It's supposed to be an adventure, but as the attic burns this doesn't feel like a game any more.

From the heart of the flames I hear the chess player laugh. He still looks like some kind of magician, but this spell that he's cast is taking us straight to Hell. The bejewelled turban has slipped from his head, exposing a melting skull beneath, but the pinned black pearl still gleams red. This must mean the camera's still filming. The Host can see what's going on.

"Something's gone wrong!" I shout, screaming straight down the camera lens. "You've got to let us out!"

But the chess player just grins as the flames consume him.

"Come on, Ami," Ibrahim yells, pulling at my arm to drag me away. Reluctantly I follow his lead, threading my way through the piles of electronic junk as the fire takes hold. On the other side of the attic Min is already crouching over the hatch. I can see scorch marks on the sleeve of her denim jacket as she strains to pull the trapdoor open.

"It's no use," she says, meeting my gaze. "It's still locked!" Beneath the dark line of her fringe, I glimpse a flicker of fear darting across Min's face. "We must have missed something."

The siren is still screaming in my ear as I look around, trying to work out what that could be. Black smoke streams across the ceiling, the acrid taste making me choke. The far end of the attic is now an inferno. Bright orange flames lick at the stacked computer monitors, the flickering numbers on their screens still counting down even while the plastic bubbles and burns.

73... 72... 71... 70...

Turning away from the spreading flames, I see Adjoa standing in front of a chunky desktop computer that looks like it's escaped from the 1980s. Its green screen shows the same numbers counting down.

66... 65... 64... 63...

"What are you doing?" I ask as she frantically taps at its keys.

"I'm trying to stop the countdown," she says, her fingers clacking across the keyboard without a pause. "I need to hack the code to find a way in, but nothing's working so far."

I'm just about to ask what I can do to help, when Oscar pushes in front of me. He grabs hold of the computer before ripping the keyboard away from Adjoa.

"There's no time to find a way in," he shouts as he throws the whole lot on the floor. "We've got to find a way out."

The monitor explodes as it hits the ground.

"You idiot!" Adjoa shouts, turning towards him

in fury. "What do you think you're doing?"

"What we should've done from the start," Oscar replies, crunching his trainer down on the computer keyboard. Its casing cracks, spitting keys across the floor. "Taking this place apart."

I stare at him in disbelief. Oscar seems to think that smashing things up will help us to escape, but the numbers scrolling across the countless computer screens behind him tell a different story. Through the haze of smoke I count them down.

49... 48... 47... 46...

What happens when they reach zero?

As Oscar and Adjoa continue to bicker, I glance back at the searing brightness of the fire. It looks like it's alive; the crackling sheets of flame leaping from floor to ceiling as they engulf the stacks of computer equipment. Every breath that I take burns the back of my throat, the billowing smoke hiding the rest of the attic from view. I want to run, but there's no way out.

"We need to find an extinguisher," I yell, shouting over Oscar and Adjoa's bickering voices. "We've got to put this fire out!"

Close by, the walnut casing of a vintage computer system spontaneously bursts into flames. The sudden heat is so intense I have to turn away. I catch sight of Ibrahim, head bent as he rummages through the toppling boxes of tech. Wires and cables spill on to the floor, circuit boards scattering as he searches for something to save our lives.

"Look at this!" he shouts, turning round to face me.

I'm desperately hoping to see a fire extinguisher, but all he's holding is an electronic device. It looks like some kind of handheld games console, but its grey plastic case doesn't make it look much fun.

"What is it?" I ask as Min crowds round too.

"It's a chess computer," Ibrahim says, holding the device out towards me. "And it's playing your game."

Two sets of rubberised buttons flank a grey-and-green LCD screen, the name of the handheld console written above this in faded red letters.

e-CHESS 2000

As I take hold of the device, I see chess pieces flickering across its pixelated screen, the moves that they're making eerily familiar. White pawn to D4, black pawn to D5, white knight to C3, black pawn takes white. Ibrahim's right – this is the same game I played when I beat the automaton, the match that lit the fire that's burning the attic down.

Standing at my shoulder, Min gasps in excitement.

"You can play the game again," she says as black and white knights flicker across the board.

I nod my head, my eyes flicking over the game's controls. LAST PIECE, LAST MOVE, NEXT PIECE, NEXT MOVE. I press down on the D–pad to try to select the next piece.

"But this time I can make sure I lose."

My finger flicks to the NEXT MOVE button, trying to force my king into play, but instead I see my bishop slide across the board. This is the exact same move I made before. I push hard on the buttons, but nothing seems to work. It's like the computer won't let me play. I watch the black and white pieces flickering across the screen, every move that's made already pre-ordained. I know how this game ends and there's nothing I can do to stop it.

"It's no use," I say, glancing up to meet Min's gaze. Her dark eyes shine with the same fear that haunts mine. "It won't let me change the past."

Behind Min, a teetering stack of computer equipment collapses with a crash. Oscar is still smashing the place up while Adjoa screams at him to stop. Sweat drips from Ibrahim's face as he stares in horror at the solid wall of flames that's bearing down on us. Through wreaths of smoke I can see the melting plastic machinery, the relentless countdown continuing across every splintered screen.

33... 32... 31... 30...

I can't think. I can't breathe. Dad said this was a game, but it feels like the end of everything.

"There must be something that we're missing," Ibrahim shouts, his voice strained above the roar of the flames. "We're looking at this the wrong way."

I glance down at the e-CHESS 2000, the same game still playing over and over again. The game controls are on the right, but along the left-hand side of the screen are four more buttons: SETUP, SHIFT, HINT, ESC. Ibrahim says there's something we're missing. We just need a clue to work out what it is.

I jab my thumb down on the HINT key and watch as a message starts to scroll across the game's LCD screen.

FIND THE ANSWER. SAVE THE WORLD.
FIND THE ANSWER. SAVE THE WORLD.

As the message scrolls, I can still see the black and white pieces moving across the digital chessboard. The game won't stop playing and this hint doesn't help. We already know we're supposed to save the world, but right now we just need to save ourselves.

"Keep trying," Min says as Oscar scrambles towards the hatch.

I jab my thumb against the button again and watch the message change.

THE CLOCK IS TICKING.
THE COUNTDOWN HAS BEGUN.

That's what the Host told us before we stepped into this place. I glance up to see the fire all around us now, the scrolling numbers still counting down as the screens melt.

14... 13... 12... 11...

There's no time left. There's no way out.

"Ami!" Adjoa shouts, her voice frantic amidst the flames. "Do something!"

I press down on the HINT key again, but the message stays the same. It's like the Host is mocking us now. I rack my brains, trying to figure out what to do next, but all I hear are his words rattling round inside my head.

The clock is ticking – the countdown has begun. Everything is part of the game. All you need to succeed is hidden inside The Escape.

Oscar pounds on the locked hatch as the numbers count down.

10... 9... 8... 7...

I stare down at the chess machine, my gaze flicking across its buttons as I search for what we've missed. And then I see it.

ESC

Escape.

The answer is staring me in the face. *All you need to succeed is hidden inside The Escape.*

5... 4... 3... 2...

I jab down hard against the ESCAPE key, feeling the rubber squish beneath my thumb.

The siren blare suddenly cuts into silence and then I hear a loud clanking noise.

"It's opening," Oscar shouts, lifting the trapdoor hatch, as we hear a sound like a giant metallic snake slithering into a well. We all crowd round the hatch, peering down into the darkness as Oscar lowers himself over the edge.

"There's a ladder here," he says, his head and shoulders slowly vanishing from view as he starts to descend. As soon as Oscar's head's clear, Min lowers herself over the edge, the clatter of her steps ringing out as she disappears too. Ibrahim's next with Adjoa following close behind.

I look around. Everything's burning. I'm still holding the e-CHESS 2000, its LCD screen now frozen in a stalemate.

"Come on, Ami!"

At the sound of Adjoa's shout I toss the computer into the flames. Then lowering myself on to the ladder, I pull the hatch closed over my head and start climbing down into the darkness.

6

Beneath my fingers, the metal feels greasy to the touch as I reach from rung to rung, my foot half slipping as I take another step down. I can't see a thing as I descend; the darkness that surrounds me absolute.

Nobody's said a word since we left the burning attic behind. The only thing that tells me that I'm not alone in the dark is the clatter of footsteps I can hear beneath me, their juddering vibrations making the ladder sway back and forth.

It feels like we've been climbing down for ever.

Peering into the inky blackness, I think I can see a faint glimmer of light below. This dimness starts to grow as I scramble down the rungs, a glowing circle of light pooling at the base of the ladder. I can see the others clustered round this: Oscar, Adjoa, Ibrahim and Min, their faces peering up as I clamber down the last few rungs.

The ladder doesn't quite reach all the way to the ground, so I have to jump the final stretch. A cloud of dust rises up as my feet hit the floor, the thud of my landing echoing away into the darkness.

"You made it," Adjoa says, smiling with relief as she reaches out a hand to help me up. "We all got out of there."

But before I can even open my mouth to reply, a harsh clanking drowns out everything else. The noise is coming from directly overhead; the metal ladder is being wound back up again, its rungs disappearing into the darkness.

I look around at the others. We might have escaped the fire, but as I try to peer beyond the circle of light that surrounds us I don't know what we're supposed to do next.

"Where are we?" Oscar growls. "I can't see a thing down here."

As if in reply to his question, the light seems to brighten, pushing back against the gloom to reveal exactly where we are standing.

"Oh, wow."

It looks like we're in some kind of library, but one bigger than I've ever seen in my life. A labyrinth of shelves stretch out in every direction: dark wooden stacks that reach from floor to ceiling, all lined with endless rows of books. I can't see where the light is coming from and, as I crane my neck to peer into the heights of the nearest stack, I realise I can't even see the ceiling. The silent shelves seem to stretch into infinity. It looks like the books go on forever.

I catch Min's gaze as I glance back at the others, the hint of a smile creeping across her lips.

"Well, it looks like we've come to the right place," she says, walking towards a large hexagonal desk that stands at the centre of the stacks. It reminds me in a strange way of the reception desk I saw when I first entered The Escape. But where the lines of that low round desk were clean and white, this dark wooden desk stands chest high, its six sides covered in a layer of grime.

"What do you mean?" Oscar snaps. He kicks up clouds of dust as he follows Min towards the central desk. "That electronic junkyard upstairs was more interesting than a stupid library. I want some action and adventure, not a bedtime story."

"Don't you see?" Min says, gesturing towards the groaning bookshelves. "Whatever the question is, we'll find the Answer in the library. We just need to find the right book."

I look around at the cavernous stacks. Staring down the nearest aisle of shelves I can't even see where they come to an end. And there are dozens of these gloomy passageways stretching out to all points of the compass. There must be hundreds of thousands of books in this place. Millions, maybe...

"And it looks like we're expected," Ibrahim calls out, reaching across the dusty desk to pick up a handful of cards. He offers these to each of us in turn and, taking mine, I look down to see my name picked out in bright white letters against a jet-black background.

Ami Oswald

Bibliothèque Universelle

ユニバーサルライブラリ

"Why've you given me this?" Oscar asks, strumming his black plastic card against his fingertips.

"It's your library card," Ibrahim explains, holding up his own so we can see we've all got the same. "Bibliothèque Universelle – the Universal Library. If we're meant to find a book, then maybe these will help us."

"I don't need a stupid library card," Oscar replies, shoving his into the pocket of his zip top. "We don't even know if we're looking for a book. There might be a secret passageway or something hidden away in this place. We just need to start exploring."

Turning away from the desk, Oscar starts to stride towards the nearest stack, his trainers kicking up fresh clouds of dust.

"Who's coming with me?" he calls out.

Glancing across at the others, I see Adjoa roll her eyes. It doesn't look like Oscar has learned anything from the mess we made of things upstairs. One of Dad's catchphrases pops into my head, the one he always says whenever he's trying to teach me something and I treat it like a race and end up making a mistake.

Fools rush in where angels fear to tread.

And now I know what he means.

"Wait a second!" I call out, stopping Oscar in his tracks. "We need to work out a plan first before we make any more mistakes."

"And whose fault is that?" Oscar snaps, turning towards me with a sneer. "It was your mistake that turned that chess player into a roman candle."

"That's what I mean," I say, trying to hide my annoyance at the way Oscar's pinning all the blame on me. "We thought we were doing the right thing, but by rushing to play the game we messed things up. We only just got out of that room alive."

"When you're playing an escape game, everything can be a clue," Min says, backing me up. "These library cards have got our names on them. They must mean something."

I glance down at mine again, turning the card over in my hand. There's a barcode on the back, the strip of black parallel lines framed in a white panel. My mind races. Barcodes are used to store information. Maybe the clue that we need is hidden inside these parallel lines.

"Have you seen this?" I say, holding up my card to show the others. "If we're meant to use these cards, then we need to find a card reader."

My gaze flicks back to the imposing desk. There's no librarian there to help us. No sign either of any of the computers they use to check out your books. Just a thick layer of dust that shows that nobody's been here for years.

"Over here!"

Adjoa's shout makes me spin round. She's heading in the opposite direction to Oscar, marching towards another of the long avenues of books. But, as I watch, Adjoa stops at what looks like a signpost that's half hidden in the shadows cast by the towering stack.

We race over to see what she's found, dust swirling beneath our feet as we reach the signpost.

At least, I thought it was a signpost, but close up I realise it's some kind of information point. A black metal column rises from a broad circular base. It reaches about three metres tall, spindly cylindrical arms branching off near the top to point in different directions. But my eyes are drawn to the display that's embedded halfway up the pillar at head height. As the others crowd round the machine, I peer over Adjoa's shoulder to read the message on the curved screen.

WELCOME TO THE LIBRARY
PLEASE SCAN YOUR CARD

Adjoa places her library card in the empty space that's located directly below the display. I watch as the thin red line of a laser beam slithers across the barcode on the back of the card and then see the message on the screen change.

WELCOME, ADJOA
YOU HAVE ONE RESERVATION
PLEASE HEAD TO YOUR COLLECTION POINT

Above my head, I hear a whirring sound and, glancing up, see one of the cylindrical arms spinning round. It comes to a sudden stop, the spindly finger on the end of this pole now pointing down one of the nearest avenues of shelves. At the end of this bookstack a brass lantern glimmers into life, the light it casts illuminating a sign that reads: THIS WAY TO COLLECTION POINT A.

Adjoa grins.

"That's A for Adjoa," she says, pocketing her library card and turning to face the rest of us. "Well, I know where I've got to go. You need to scan your cards too to see if this gives us any more clues."

I'm the closest to the machine, but before I can even get my card ready, Oscar barges in ahead of me.

"Get out of the way," he snaps, shouldering me to one side as he scans his card. "If we need a stupid book to find the Answer, then I'm going to be the first one to find it."

A new welcome message appears on the screen as, with a whirr, another metallic arm above our heads starts to turn.

WELCOME, OSCAR
YOU HAVE ONE RESERVATION
PLEASE HEAD TO YOUR COLLECTION POINT

When it comes to a stop, the arm is pointing in the opposite direction. I turn round to see a lantern now shining at the entrance to another long avenue of books. Beneath its glow, I can just make out some words, written in gold: THIS WAY TO COLLECTION POINT O.

"It's the same way I was going before," Oscar grunts, flashing me a look. "Told you I had the right idea."

I stare at him, astounded. If it wasn't for me, Oscar wouldn't even know he was looking for a book. While I'm still thinking of a sarcastic comeback, Ibrahim and Min take it in turns to scan their cards. The message on the screen tells them both the same thing.

YOU HAVE ONE RESERVATION
PLEASE HEAD TO YOUR COLLECTION POINT

The metallic arms slowly revolve, pointing Ibrahim one way and Min the other. I realise now why I thought this information point was a signpost at first; its cylindrical poles point to the four corners of the library. It's like whoever made these reservations wants to split us up.

"Go on, Ami," Adjoa says. "It's your turn now."

Placing my card into position, I watch the laser beam scroll across the barcode, then look up to see the fresh message on the screen.

WELCOME, AMI
YOU HAVE 129,864,880 BOOKS OVERDUE
YOUR ACCOUNT HAS BEEN SUSPENDED

This can't be right.

I scan the card again, thinking the machine must have made some kind of mistake, but the message stays the same.

Leaning over my shoulder, Adjoa lets out a low whistle. "That's going to be a *monumental* fine."

I don't understand. I've never been to this library before, let alone borrowed millions of books. This doesn't make any sense. It's impossible.

I take my library card out from under the scanner and rub the barcode on the back of my sleeve. Maybe there's a speck of dust on it that's made the card reader go haywire. I place the card back in the empty space below the screen and watch as the thin red line of the laser rolls across the barcode again.

Nothing changes. This machine still thinks I've borrowed 129 million books and it's telling me they're all overdue.

"Well, I've not got time to hang around with you losers," Oscar says, starting to stride towards the stacks. "I've got the Answer to find and I'll be back here before you've even worked out what the question is."

We watch him go, the tread of his trainers leaving

footprints in the dust as he heads down the lantern-lit passageway of books.

Min turns to the rest of us. "Oscar's right," she says. "We need to collect our reservations."

Ibrahim nods his head, but I feel my face flushing red.

It's not fair. Everyone else has got a mission — a reservation to collect from somewhere inside this Universal Library — but my account's been suspended. How am I supposed to find the Answer if I can't even play the game?

"Don't worry, Ami," Adjoa says, sensing my disappointment. "You can come with me. I could use some help finding my way in this place."

Her mouth crinkles into a smile as I nod my head gratefully.

I know she's only saying it to be nice, but I can't help feeling kind of relieved that I'm not going to be left on my own. There's something a tiny bit creepy about this deserted library.

"We'll meet back here as soon as we've found the reservations," Ibrahim says, still holding on to his library card. "I know Oscar thinks he's going to find the Answer on his own, but there must be a reason we've all got our own cards."

I glance back at the information point; my account suspended message still displayed on the screen. I don't know how this fits into Ibrahim's theory. Maybe it's the Host's way of letting me know he doesn't like the way I play.

Lifting my head, I look beyond to where the brass lantern lights the way to Collection Point A. As Ibrahim and Min set off in opposite directions, Adjoa and I start walking towards our own aisle in this vast cathedral of books.

It's time to explore the library.

7

"What do you think of the others?" Adjoa asks, our footsteps echoing as we walk along the gloomy corridor of books.

Motes of dust dance in the eerie glow cast by the lanterns fixed at the end of each gallery of shelves. Each lantern only flickers into life when we reach the start of the next row. It's as if the library doesn't want us to see what lies ahead.

"I don't know," I say, feeling distracted by Adjoa's question as I strain my eyes against the gloom. "What do *you* think of them?"

"I like Ibrahim," Adjoa replies without missing a beat. "I like the way he looks at things. The way he found that chess computer and the library cards too. You need someone like him on your team. A *finder*. Someone who can see the things that everyone else has missed."

I nod my head. What Adjoa's saying makes sense. If it hadn't been for Ibrahim's spotting skills, we'd still be stuck in that burning attic. At the back of my neck I feel my skin start to prickle as I remember the roar of the flames. I still can't believe that the Host nearly turned us into toast.

"Min's the clever one," Adjoa continues, counting off the others on the fingers of her left hand. "Just look at the way she knew all about that Chess-Player of Marzipan or whatever it was called. She's always scribbling things down in that notebook of hers. If you ask me, she's the brains of this team."

I can't help feeling a bit miffed that Adjoa reckons Min's cleverer than me. After all, *I* was the one who worked out that we needed to press the ESCAPE key to get out of the attic. But there's no point in reminding Adjoa of this as she's already moved on to letting me know what she thinks of Oscar.

"We're just unlucky we've ended up with someone like *him*," she says. The way she spits out this last word makes it perfectly clear who she's talking about. "In an escape room some players are good at finding clues, others are skilled at solving puzzles, but some people just like to move fast and break things. That's what Oscar does. He's your classic *destroyer*. He'll use brute force rather than his brains every time. We'll just have to try to keep him on a short leash to stop him from wrecking the game for the rest of us."

The next lantern flickers into life, illuminating the galleries ahead that look just like all the rest. A sliding ladder is fastened close to the wall, its wooden rungs offering access to the out-of-reach shelves, but as I glance up into the heights of the stack I don't think anyone would dare to climb to the top.

"What about me?" I ask, turning my gaze back towards Adjoa. "What do I bring to the team?"

Folding her arms across her chest, Adjoa makes a show of sizing me up.

"A bit of everything, I think. You're clever like Min, good at spotting things just like Ibrahim and you're not scared to stand up to Oscar too." A mischievous smile creeps across her lips. "I reckon that makes you team captain."

I feel myself blush, a sudden warmth blooming across my cheeks.

"No, thanks," I say, brushing Adjoa's compliments away with a shake of my head. "We don't need a team captain."

Adjoa looks like she's ready to argue the point, so I quickly change the subject by throwing the question back at her.

"How about you?" I ask as another brass lantern flickers into life to light the path ahead. "What are your special skills?"

"Me?" Adjoa grins. "I'm this team's secret weapon. Think Lara Croft meets Indiana Jones, but with a better sense of style. Deadly pit with snakes in it? No problem. Falling swords and rolling boulders? Bring them on. Booby-trapped statue? Just give me a shout. I'm a natural-born adventurer. This game was made for me.

"Come on," she says, quickening her step as we continue our trek down the avenue of books. "We don't want the others to beat us to all the fun stuff."

It's strange to think of the others, somewhere in this library, all searching for the same thing. As

Adjoa hurries ahead, I trail my finger along one of the shelves, skimming over the leather-bound spines that sit there tightly packed. A musty smell hangs in the air, the scent making me feel as if I'm breathing in the books themselves. In the glow from the lantern I read the titles on the spines, each one picked out in golden letters: *Do Glaciers Listen? Can a Submarine Swim? Why Don't Things Fall Down?* We're supposed to be looking for the Answer, but all I can see here are stupid questions.

Pausing for a second, I take one of the books down from the shelf. Its red-leather binding is scuffed with age, but at least the cracked letters of its title aren't asking another question.

EXPRESSION OF THE EMOTIONS
by Charles Darwin

It looks like one of those old-fashioned books that Dad's always trying to get me to read. Ones that he thinks will improve my mind. Like that time he gave me the complete works of William Shakespeare and then got annoyed when he caught me reading a walkthrough for *The Legend of Zelda*. He says I need to broaden my horizons, but I don't see why I can't do that in a video game.

Flicking through its pages, the book falls open at a photograph: a sepia-tinged picture of a baby, her eyes all screwed up and her mouth open wide. It looks like she's crying, her face captured mid-scream, but as I stare at the picture I start to think that maybe she's laughing instead.

It's like two opposite emotions are captured in the same photograph. The expressions look so similar to me. The baby screams, but is it with joy or despair? Absent-mindedly I brush my fingertip across the photograph and gasp as I feel a teardrop rolling down the page.

I stare at the baby openmouthed, trying to work out if this is real, and then I see a line of text appearing beneath the picture…

Do you know how it feels to feel, Ami?

I slam the book shut, sending a fresh shower of dust to the floor. The words were printed on the page but it was like I could hear them in my head. It sounded like the Host himself, whispering in my ear.

"Ami!"

Adjoa's shout pulls me out of my fear. Quickly sliding the book back on to the shelf, I turn round to see her, some twenty metres ahead. She's standing directly beneath another brass-bound lantern, the eerie light it casts showing me a solid wall of empty shelves.

It's a dead end.

My heart starts to sink, thinking we've come the wrong way, but then Adjoa steps to one side to reveal a sign.

WELCOME TO COLLECTION POINT A

"We're here," she says.

8

"But where's the book?" I ask, desperately searching the shelves for any sign of the reservation that should be waiting for us.

"I don't know," Adjoa replies, her hands and knees grimed with dust as she climbs to her feet after checking the bottom shelf. "It must be here somewhere."

I look back over my shoulder. The towering stacks that lined our path are now shrouded in darkness again. The only light still shining comes from the lantern that's fixed above the sign welcoming us to Collection Point A.

But as I turn back to inspect the empty shelves that mark the end of this blind alley, I still can't see anything for us to collect.

"Maybe the library machine got it wrong," I say, remembering the millions of overdue books it said I'd borrowed. "Maybe this wasn't where we were supposed to go."

Lifting her gaze, Adjoa peers at the countless shelves that stretch up out of reach.

"We haven't looked everywhere yet."

Another sliding ladder rests at the far end of this empty bookcase, but as I wait for Adjoa to spring into action, she turns to me instead.

"Can you find it, Ami?"

I glance down to see she's holding out her library card for me to take.

I shake my head, thinking that she's just trying to be nice to me again.

"It's your reservation," I say, gently pushing her hand away. "Not mine. You should be the one to find it."

But Adjoa seems to wince at my refusal, a pained look flitting across her face. She casts a nervous glance towards the ladder, its wooden rungs covered in a thin layer of dust.

"I–I can't," she says, stuttering out her reply. "I just can't."

I feel confused. Up until now, Adjoa's been the one leading the way, but she seems to have frozen on me. And then she tells me why.

"I'm scared of heights."

I look at her askance. "How can you be scared of heights?" I ask, struggling to hide my incredulity. "You climbed down that ladder from the attic and that felt like it was a mile high."

"That was different," Adjoa says, pouting slightly. "I couldn't see where I was in the dark." She glances up again at the endless shelves, all lit by an eerie glow. "Not like now."

Holding out her card again, she meets my gaze plaintively. "Please, Ami. Find it for me."

Adjoa said she was a natural-born adventurer, just like Indiana Jones, but it looks like her secret fear is heights not snakes.

Taking the library card, I slip this into my pocket next to mine.

"OK," I say, reaching for the ladder. "But there's no guarantee I'll find anything up there. This whole thing might just be a red herring."

"Thanks, skipper," Adjoa says, a relieved smile

breaking across the shoreline of her face. "I owe you one."

The wooden rungs creak in protest as I start to climb.

"I'll hold the ladder," she says, stationing herself at the bottom as soon as my legs are clear. "Don't worry about it coming away from the wall."

"I wasn't," I mutter as I reach for the next rung. "Not until you mentioned it."

Looking up, I can see a sheer wall of shelf edges stretching up towards the ceiling. Just like all the other stacks, I can't see where this one ends; the highest of the ledges disappear into the darkness. The ladder seems to tremble as I hoist myself up towards the next.

That's the thing about fear. It's infectious.

Lowering my gaze, I hold on to the ladder a little more tightly as I peer along the length of the shelf straight ahead. There's no need to look up or down, I can just keep my eyes fixed in front of me, searching one shelf at a time as I climb. But every dusty shelf that I peer down is empty; no sign anywhere of Adjoa's reservation.

Dust crumbles beneath my fingers as I climb. It doesn't look like anyone has been up this ladder for years, so how can a reservation be waiting for us here?

"I can't see anything," I shout, half hoping that Adjoa will just say to give up now.

No such luck.

"Keep on looking," she calls out, her voice sounding further away than I thought it would be. "Remember everything could be part of the game. Even these empty shelves could be hiding a secret. I know you'll find something, Ami. I can feel it in my bones."

A bead of sweat forms on my brow as I hear this echo of the Host. *Everything is part of the game*. I remember the book that I found with the picture of the baby, its tear seeming to run down the page. The words I read there seem to whisper again inside my brain. *Do you know how it feels to feel, Ami?*

I nod my head as I keep on climbing. I feel scared.

The Host said he'd be monitoring our every move. But in the first room of this game he almost left us to die in the flames. The ladder shakes as I reach for the next rung. If he's watching now, will he catch me if I fall?

I don't dare look down to see how far I've climbed. I just keep on searching, one shelf at a time. Some are labelled with a single word scribbled inside a brass holder and fixed to the edge of the shelf: ZOOLOGY, PHILOSOPHY, SCIENCE, HISTORY and more. All human knowledge, classified and organised inside the library. Min thought we'd find the Answer here, but each label I see catalogues only a thick layer of dust. The shelves are empty.

Pausing for a second, I glance up to see how far I've got left to climb. The stack stretches up into the darkness, the sheer wall of shelves looking just as steep as before. My heart sinks. What's the point of climbing up if I never reach the top?

Then I see it, a slim volume lying on its side, nearly pushed out of sight in a dark corner of the shelf. Keeping a tight grip on the ladder with one hand, I reach across to pick up the book. It's covered in a thick layer of dust, but, as I brush this off, I can read the title etched, in golden-green letters, on its cover.

A Natural Treasury

A buzz of excitement starts to thrum through my brain. This must be it.

I know I should head down the ladder straight away to show Adjoa what I've found. It's her reservation, after all. But I can't resist opening the book to see what it's about. In the gloom of the shelf I can just about read these jagged lines.

There is another sky,
Ever serene and fair,
And there is another sunshine,
Though it be darkness there;
Never mind faded forests,
Never mind silent fields—
Here is a little forest,
Whose leaf is ever green...

But as I try to read the remaining lines, the words seem to slip from the page. I watch astounded as the black ink turns to dust and, as I let out a gasp of surprise, these specks are blown into the air. I stare down at the book, the page now a blank sheet of whiteness.

Feeling sick, I start to flick through the book, thinking that somehow I've made a mistake. But every page just spills out a fresh fountain of dust and, as I strain my eyes against the gloom, I see they're *all* blank now.

I don't know how this can be happening, but as I rack my brain for an explanation, I notice that it seems so much darker than before. I look up, trying to work out why, and feel the fear rise in my throat.

Darkness seems to be falling out of the sky, but then I realise.

It's not darkness. It's dust.

9

"Did you find it?" Adjoa asks, her eager voice bubbling in my ear as soon as my feet hit the floor.

Turning round, I reach for the book in my pocket, my knuckles still white from where they were gripping the ladder.

"I found this," I tell her, handing over the slim leather-bound text.

Adjoa starts to flick through the book, her excited smile undimmed by the gloom. But as she turns the pages, this smile starts to fade before she stops to look up at me with a questioning gaze.

"It's blank," she says, a puzzled frown

furrowing her brow. "There's nothing written inside."

My heart thuds in my chest. "There was something," I say, struggling to explain exactly what I saw. "It was a poem, I think. But as I read it, the words just turned into dust. Every page was the same. It was like the book was being erased."

Even as I speak it seems to be getting darker. Reaching out, I hold out my hand and watch the dust landing there. Each speck seems to gleam in the glow cast by the lantern light and, as I glance up, I see the dust still falling like rain. Where's this coming from?

A terrible thought creeps into my head. Turning away, I head towards the darkened stacks; their tightly packed shelves are a stark contrast to the empty dead end of Collection Point A. With a mounting sense of dread I pull out a handful of books and watch them spill across the floor. Across scuffed leather covers, the gold gilt letters of their titles seem to spell out a message to me: *What Have We Done*; *Our Final Warning*; *This Changes Everything*.

"What are you doing?" Adjoa calls out.

But as I crouch to flick through their pages, my

answer sticks in my throat. Swirls of soot rise like mist from the empty books, every page the same. Blinking, I cough, waving my hand to clear the air, but when I look down, the pages are blank. There are no words left, only dust.

A shadow falls and I look up to see Adjoa standing over me. Her smile has gone and I see the same look of fear in her eyes that I feel inside.

"Something bad is happening here," I say, clambering to my feet. "We've got to get back."

We start to run, retracing our steps along this dark avenue of books. One by one, the brass lanterns flicker into life as we pass, but the light they cast now seems shrouded in shadows. Black specks dance in front of my eyes as I see the footprints we left slowly disappearing beneath a curtain of dust. I pull the collar of my T-shirt up, covering my mouth and nose.

"Maybe this is coming from the fire in the attic," Adjoa says, spluttering for breath as we run.

I shake my head, finding it hard to breathe too. "It's the books."

It feels like we've been running for ever, our pounding steps sending up fresh clouds of dust. When we first walked down this corridor, books were lined neatly on the shelves, stretching as far as the eye could see. But now as we run I can see them scattered everywhere. It looks like the place has been ransacked, the books torn from the shelves and strewn across the floor. Everything is covered in a layer of dust that's getting thicker by the second.

I peer ahead into the gathering gloom and see the gap between the towering stacks begin to widen. We must be nearing the place where we started. I can hear voices in the distance, the sound getting louder as we run. I only hope the others have had more luck than us.

"Ami!"

I hear Ibrahim's shout as we burst into the open and I turn to see him standing in the shadow of the information point. Oscar's there too, staring at the screen; the spindly arms that branch off its trunk offer no shelter from the dust that's falling all around.

"Did you find it?" Ibrahim asks as Adjoa and I try to catch our breath.

He's holding a book and I recognise it straight away.

A Natural Treasury

It's the same book that I found at Collection Point A.

Adjoa pulls our copy from her pocket. "We found it," she says, flicking through the book to show Ibrahim its empty pages. "But it doesn't tell us anything."

"Mine's the same," Ibrahim says. "When I first opened it, I thought I saw something written inside, but the words just seemed to turn into dust."

I remember pulling the book from the shadows of the shelf. There were words written in Adjoa's too, their jagged lines seared into my memory.

The sound of Oscar slamming his fist against the screen shatters my concentration. Turning round, he brandishes the same book.

"It's useless," he shouts. "I've tried scanning this book a million times, but the stupid machine keeps telling me the same thing."

Peering over his shoulder, I read the message that's displayed on the screen.

RESERVATION NOT RECOGNISED
PLEASE TRY AGAIN

"These books are a waste of time," he growls. "I knew Min was talking rubbish when she said we'd find the Answer here."

"Where is Min?" I ask, suddenly realising that we're not all here.

"I don't know," Ibrahim says. "We split up, remember."

The library seems to growl in reply, a low, rumbling sound that shakes the air. I glance up at the seething cloud above our heads, a swirling mass of dust that's getting darker by the second. As the falling specks land on my lips I feel a strange sensation shudder through me and quickly wipe the dust away.

"This is bad," Adjoa shouts, raising her voice above the clamour. "This is really bad."

I look around, seeing the dark hexagonal desk still unmanned in the centre of the library. There's no librarian standing there ready to shush us. I don't know what we're supposed to do now. All I can think is that we've got to get out.

I crane my neck, trying to peer down the labyrinth of shelves. And then I see Min stumble clear of the stacks.

10

Min staggers towards us, her face grey with dust.

I just manage to reach her before she falls to the floor and I feel her dead weight sag in my arms.

"Is she OK?" Ibrahim asks, racing to my side to help me drag Min into a sitting position, leaning against the library desk.

"I don't know," I say as I watch her eyelids flutter.

Oscar appears at my shoulder. "Did she find anything?" he says. "Did she find the book?"

Adjoa starts to shush him, but then

Min opens her eyes wide.

"I found the book," she replies, the words escaping from her lips in a giggle. "I found so many books. Big books, little books, true books and lies. And I ate them all up."

Min giggles again and then sticks her tongue out at us. I see with a shudder that it's stained black with dust.

A fresh peal of thunder crashes through the library, the sound rolling down the stacks. I rest my hand on Min's shoulder, leaning close to find out what's gone wrong. "What happened, Min?"

Her eyes blink again and then open wide as if seeing me for the first time.

"It hurts," she says, her voice trembling as she reaches up to touch the side of her head. "In here. It's like the dust is talking to me."

She looks like a grey ghost as she stares up at me with haunted eyes. "I thought I'd find the Answer, but all I can see is darkness." Then Min starts coughing and I think she's never going to stop.

It's getting darker by the second; the blackened air is so thick that I'm finding it hard to breathe.

"What about the books?" Adjoa calls out, her voice almost lost in the deluge. "There must be something we can do."

Shielding my eyes, I stare up into the darkness, feeling hopeless. All the books in the world can't save us now. It's their words that are choking us.

But as I stare up into this sky of dust, some words are shaken loose inside my head.

There is another sky…

Dust rolls like thunder down the stacks, but I grab hold of these words. This means something.

"We need to use our minds," I shout, turning round to face the others. In their hands, Ajdoa, Oscar and Ibrahim still hold *A Natural Treasury* and I reach out to snatch the slim volume from Adjoa's grasp. "I thought I saw a poem inside this book, but it must have been a puzzle. If we can solve it, then we'll find the way out."

"What did it say?" Ibrahim asks, his voice muffled as he covers his mouth with his sleeve. "The words in my book disappeared before I could even read them."

Flicking through the book, it falls open at the same place as before. The page is blank, but I can still see the words inside my head as I recite them out loud.

"There is another sky,
Ever serene and fair,
And there is another sunshine,
Though it be darkness there;
Never mind faded forests,
Never mind silent fields—
Here is a little forest,
Whose leaf is ever green…"

I look up from the page to see darkness everywhere. Shadows spill from the heights of the towering stacks, books floating like flotsam in this relentless avalanche of dust. The swirling air is thick with choking specks, the sharp taste stinging my throat. We're trapped in a library of dust and I don't know what this puzzle means.

I hear Ibrahim muttering, the sound all but lost in the tumult.

"Here is a little forest, whose leaf is ever green…"

His eyes seem to gleam as he reaches the end of the line. Turning towards me, he raises his hands to the sky.

"This is the forest," Ibrahim shouts, gesturing around at the labyrinth of shelves. "Think about it. What else is a library but a forest of books?" He holds up his own book, its pages flickering open as the dust rains down. "And inside every book are the leaves."

I stare at Ibrahim astounded. He's found the key to unlock the puzzle, but I still don't know what we have to do.

Half blinded by the dust, I look around in desperation. Through the choking haze my gaze falls on the information point, its strange metal structure rocked by the oncoming storm. As I stare at this, each jagged breath rasping in my lungs, I suddenly realise that it reminds me of something else. The broad trunk with its spindly arms branching off in every direction. The shape of a tree.

And that's what we need to breathe.

I look down at the book in my hands. "Every book was a tree once," I shout, raising my voice above the thunder of dust. "And that's what we need now. We're choking to death and trees make the oxygen we breathe. We need to build a tree."

"That's the stupidest thing I've ever heard," Oscar sneers, his face set into a snarl as the darkness falls. "How are we supposed to build a tree?"

Min coughs again and I glance down to see that she's holding something out to me. It's a page she's torn from her book, but she's folded it into a new shape. It looks like a leaf, its crisp edges pinched to a point while its pleated stem twists between her fingertips.

"There's an old Chinese proverb," Min says, still struggling to catch her breath. "The best time to plant a tree was twenty years ago. The second best time is now."

I take the origami leaf from her, suddenly realising what we have to do.

"The tree is already here," I say, pointing towards the bare branches of the information point, the sight of this nearly lost in the storm. "All it needs are the leaves."

As the dust swirls, I sprint towards the structure, the origami leaf trembling in my hand. I can taste grit between my teeth, a fresh gale of words raging inside my head. I try to put these out of my mind, focusing on the one thing that I need to do now.

Reaching the machine, I brush a thick layer of dust from the screen, staring at the message there as the darkness rains down.

RESERVATION NOT RECOGNISED
PLEASE TRY AGAIN

With trembling fingers I place the origami leaf in the empty space beneath the display and then watch as the thin red line of the laser slithers across the folded paper. I hear a whirring noise and glancing up see one of the metallic arms start to turn as a new message appears on the screen.

RESERVATION ACCEPTED
PLEASE PLACE IN THE SLOT

It's worked. Reaching up, I grab hold of the revolving arm, scrabbling to find the thing that it's told me to search for. Then I feel it, a tiny slot notched on the cylindrical branch. Fumbling, I slide the stem of the leaf into this slot and then step back to see what happens next.

A faint gleam of sunlight seems to shine on the folded paper, a golden brightness that shimmers in the dark. The words of the puzzle poem chime inside my head. *There is another sunshine…* Then the origami leaf starts to unfold itself, the paper rustling as it slowly turns green. It's like it's remembering what it used to be – the origami shape transformed Pinocchio-like into the leaf of a real tree.

I stare at this astonished, the lone leaf shining

green as dust swirls all around. Then a new message appears on the screen.

NEXT RESERVATION PLEASE

Spinning on my heels, I turn to face the others. Min is still slumped in the shadow of the desk.

"It works!" I shout as a fresh roll of thunder crashes through the library. "We need more leaves!"

Racing back to Min, I rip a page out of my book, holding this out for her to take. Still coughing, we watch as she folds this page in half, doubling over the corners and the edges and then tucking the little flaps inside, every crease she makes transforming it into a leaf.

She looks ashen as she holds it up for me to take. "Quickly, Ami."

I race back to the information point as the others start to tear their own books apart. Scanning the paper, I get the same message again, another arm of the machine swinging round for me to slot the leaf into place. Adjoa and Ibrahim are following Min's lead, folding the torn pages from their books into origami leaves. Even Oscar seems to be joining in, a mad grin on his face as he rips the pages out.

We race back and forth to the information point, every leaf scanned and slotted in the tree. It looks more real with every passing second, the branches glistening green as they reach towards a sky still seething with dust.

Then I hear another crack of thunder, so much louder than the rest of the noise. And I watch as the dark trunk of the information point starts to open up.

"This way," Oscar shouts, scrambling towards the widening crack. "There's a way out."

As the dust swirls, I watch him squeeze through the gap, Ibrahim and Adjoa following close behind. I start to follow too, but then glance back to see Min still slumped in the shadow of the library desk.

She won't make it on her own.

I race back to Min's side, trying not to breathe in the dust as a hard rain hammers down on us both. Her eyes are closed and I have to lean close to check that she's still breathing.

"Wake up, Min," I say, shaking her shoulder to try to wake her. "We've got to get out."

Min's eyelids flicker open. "I had a dream," she says, her glazed eyes staring up at me as if waking from a sleep. "I dreamed I was a butterfly."

For a second a faint smile plays across Min's lips. Then a coughing fit overtakes her. She covers her mouth with her sleeve, bending forward as these rasping barks rack her slender frame. Each hacking cough sounds as if it might be her last and when Min pulls her hand away, I see black specks on her sleeve.

With frightened eyes she stares up at me as the dust storm rages. "Now I feel like I'm a butterfly dreaming it's a girl."

"It's OK," I say. "I'm going to get you out of here."

I reach out to take Min's hand, but instead she grabs hold of my arm. Her fingernails dig into my skin as another coughing fit overtakes her.

"Don't you understand, Ami?" she says as the coughs finally subside, her words coming in shuddering gasps. "I was wrong. I wasn't dreaming before. This is the dream. I am the butterfly."

I stare at Min. What she's saying makes no sense at all. I think this dust has poisoned her mind.

"Ami!"

A shout makes me turn my head. Through a blinding hail of dust I glimpse Adjoa, her face framed by the darkened gate now cut into the base of the information point.

"You've got to get out now," she yells. "This is starting to close."

"Come on," I say, struggling to pull Min upright as I sling her arm round my shoulder. "I'm not leaving you behind."

Through the thunder of the storm I stumble towards the information point, Min a dead weight by my side. The swirling dust cuts into us like tiny daggers; each snatched breath I take scrapes at my throat. I feel myself retch, coughing out a blackened spray of phlegm as I reach the shelter of the leaves. I glimpse the dark hollow cut into the metal trunk and scramble towards it, praying there's still time to get out.

The gate is closing with a grinding noise, the vibrations shaking this strange metal tree. I go first as the gap's too narrow for us to fit through together and Adjoa reaches out to pull me through. I turn round to do the same for Min, but instead I see her take a step away.

"Come on," I shout, feeling the sides of the sharp metal start to press against my shoulders. "I can't keep it open for much longer."

Min shakes her head, her face framed by a halo of

dust. "I need to wake up," she says, taking another step backwards. "Goodbye, Ami. Please find the Answer for me."

I reach out my hand, gritting my teeth against the pain as the closing gate groans. But as my fingers brush against Min's, I feel her start to disintegrate.

"No!" I shout as Min seems to turn to dust. One moment she's there and the next she's gone as the darkness swarms around her.

I stare out in horror at the seething storm, unable to believe what I've just seen.

Then I feel myself dragged backwards, the gate closing with a clang as the ground crumbles beneath my feet.

11

Rocks tumble around me as I fall. It's like I'm caught in a landslide, pitched forward and downwards into the dark. I feel my body twist, legs desperately bicycling against empty air. I keep trying to grab hold of something in the blackness, but nothing meets my flailing hands…

BAM!

My shoulder crashes against stone, the sudden impact knocking the breath out of me. It's like I've been slammed into a brick wall and, as I lie sprawled in pain, the ground feels hard against my face.

For a moment I don't move, trying to

work out if I've broken anything. All I can hear in the darkness are my own juddering breaths. Then I see a flicker of light, which brightens with a crackle to form a spreading orange glow.

Every part of me aches as I pull myself upright, seeing the others scrambling to their feet too. We seem to be standing in some kind of chamber, the light coming from a burning torch that's fixed high on the nearest wall. The stone walls are covered in carvings, the strange figures of monsters and men looming in the gloom. Unlike the endless library of dust that we've just escaped from, this chamber is only ten metres long and maybe half as wide. In the centre of the room is what looks like a solid-stone table, the rough floor around it strewn with bones. I think they look human...

Glancing back over my shoulder, I see a vaulted stairway choked with rubble. This must be the landslide that brought us here: a wall of stone that shows there's no way out.

I turn back to face the others; the three of them are staring straight at me.

Adjoa's the first to speak.

"Where's Min?"

Her dark braids frame a look of real worry, lips

pursed as she waits for my reply. But, as I meet
Adjoa's gaze, all I can see in my mind is Min's face
turning to dust.

"She's gone," I say, struggling to speak. "I tried
to pull her back, but she didn't want to come. The
door was closing, the dust swarming everywhere. I
watched her disintegrate…"

My words trail away as I feel a tear rolling down
my face.

There's a moment of silence and then Oscar
laughs out loud. "Yeah, right," he says. "You're
such a sucker, Ami."

"What do you mean?" I say, staring back at him
in disbelief. "Didn't you hear what I said? Didn't
you see what was happening out there?"

Oscar sniffs, wiping the dust from his face with
the back of his sleeve.

"Special effects," he replies. "That's all it was.
The fire, the dust, the disappearing Min – it's all
just part of the story. This is the ultimate escape
game, remember?"

"This isn't a game," I say, raising my voice to a
shout. My gaze falls on the scattered bones and I
feel my heart twist. "I just watched Min crumble
into dust."

"That's what they want you to *think* you saw," Oscar says, brushing the dust from his hands. "Min wasn't one of us. She knew too much – just think about all those hints she gave. She was part of the game and now they've got her out of the way to see how we cope on our own."

Standing close by, Ibrahim slowly nods his head.

"I've heard that some escape rooms do this," he says. "Put a person on the team playing the game to keep tabs on them. They'll give clues if they see the team getting stuck, but they never let on that they're really an actor."

"You see," Oscar says, nodding his head in Ibrahim's direction. "He knows what I'm talking about. Don't worry about Min – she'll be safely back with the Host. They're probably watching us right now." He looks around the chamber as if searching for a hidden camera. "So we need to show them we can find the Answer on our own."

"I know what I saw," I protest as Oscar turns away. I glance across to Adjoa, looking for support, but my friend just shrugs her shoulders.

"Maybe he's right, Ami," she says.

It's like they're desperate to convince themselves that this is still a game.

I feel a flicker of doubt creep into my mind. How can I be sure that what I saw was really true? Surely Dad wouldn't have brought me here if he thought there was any chance of me getting hurt. I remember Min's fingers brushing against mine as I felt her start to disintegrate, but the clouds of dust could've hidden what was really happening. Maybe it *was* just smoke and mirrors…

"So what is this place?" Oscar's gruff question pulls me back to the present. "Some kind of ancient ruin?"

I look around the vaulted chamber, its rough stone roof not much higher than our heads. Shadows dance across the sculpted walls, the shapes of skulls and hieroglyphs hemming us in on every side. At least I know why they call this The Escape – there's no way out again.

"We're inside a Mayan temple," Adjoa says, leaning closer to inspect the stone carvings. "This is the burial chamber."

"Who's Amaya?" Oscar sneers. "And why's she buried here?"

"The *Mayans* were an ancient civilisation," Adjoa replies, ignoring the sneer in Oscar's question. "They ruled for more than a thousand years, building great cities in the forests of Mexico and Central America. And then they just disappeared, abandoning their cities as their civilisation collapsed. Their palaces and pyramids lay hidden for centuries, lost deep in the jungle, until their ruins were discovered by intrepid explorers."

"Wait a minute," Ibrahim says, raising his hand as if asking a question in class. "I thought it was the ancient Egyptians who built the pyramids."

Adjoa shakes her head. "The Mayans built pyramids too, with steep steps on every side. At the top was a temple where priests carried out human sacrifices, while inside the pyramids explorers found secret tunnels, chambers and traps. This is where we must be now: inside the heart of a Mayan pyramid."

"How do you know all this?" I ask, not sure where Adjoa is pulling all these facts from. "Were you reading *The Rough Guide to Ancient Civilisations* while I was climbing that ladder back in the library?"

Adjoa grins in reply. "The thirteenth level of *Tomb Raider: Underworld* is set in a Mayan temple," she says. "That's how I recognised these hieroglyphs. I told you this game was made for me."

Ibrahim frowns as he looks around the chamber.

"So we just need to find the secret tunnel and avoid the traps, right?"

"We need to find the Answer," Oscar says, striding towards the long stone table that's set in the middle of the floor. "So get looking."

Sticking out her tongue behind Oscar's back, Adjoa still seems to follow his order, turning away from the Mayan hieroglyphs to start searching the chamber. Pushing all thoughts of Min out of my mind, I follow her lead, looking around for any kind of clue. I think the only way out of this game is to win it.

Glancing down at the desiccated bones strewn around my feet, I recognise the shapes of ribs, femurs and vertebrae from the pages of my encyclopedia. They're definitely human. A shudder runs down my spine as I stare into the hollow eye sockets of a cracked skull as its yellowed teeth grin back at me.

"Are these the bones of the people who were buried here?" I ask, my voice echoing off the walls even though it's barely more than a whisper.

Adjoa shakes her head. "They're human sacrifices," she says, stepping over the jumbled cascade of bones. "When a Mayan noble died, their servants were killed to accompany them into the afterlife." She points to the long stone table that Oscar is now standing behind. "That's who's buried here."

Stepping closer, I realise now that it isn't a table but a sarcophagus. A solid slab of stone rests on top of the monolithic coffin, swirling patterns and hieroglyphs carved into its flagstone lid. Near the top, I see a small circular hollow and catch a glint of red deep inside this spyhole. It reminds me of the red dot I saw in the centre of the camera lens and the one that gleamed from the black pearl in the chess-player's turban. Inside my mind I hear the whisper of the Host's words again. *I will be monitoring your every move.*

Oscar was right. He's watching us now.

Leaning closer, Adjoa is already inspecting the strange carvings. The largest of these is a circle with swirling spirals set inside.

"This is the symbol of Hunab Ku," she says, her voice hushed as her fingers trace the shape. "Some say the Mayans believed he was the god who created everything."

"He should know what the Answer is then," grunts Oscar.

I'm expecting Adjoa to roll her eyes at Oscar's interruption, but instead she eagerly nods her head.

"He should," she replies, her dark eyes gleaming with excitement. "Don't you see, this means we're on the right track. The Mayans believed that Hunab Ku lived in the centre of the Milky Way – that's what this spiral shape represents, the galaxy we live in. Others call it the Galactic Butterfly. Some say the symbol of the Hunab Ku shows the gateway to all knowledge, so this must be where the Answer is."

Oscar cracks his knuckles with a grin. "Let's get the lid off this thing then."

12

"It's useless," Oscar shouts, stepping away as he wipes the sweat from his face. "You bunch of weaklings are no help at all."

We've been trying to shift this solid slab of stone for what feels like hours, the four of us straining to push the lid off the sarcophagus to reveal the contents within. But in all that time we've not managed to move it even a single centimetre. It weighs a ton.

"Says you," Adjoa snaps in reply. "Here's the one puzzle that needs brute force instead of brains and it turns out that you're all mouth."

As the two of them start to argue, I turn away with a heavy sigh. Adjoa seems convinced that the Answer lies inside this sarcophagus, but I can't shake the nagging feeling that something's not quite right. I look around the gloom of the burial chamber, peering into the flickering shadows as I try to work out what's wrong.

Ibrahim is crouching close to the floor, his head bent as he peers at something that he's found there.

"What is it?" I ask, wondering if he's feeling the same as me.

Brushing his dark hair away from his face, Ibrahim glances up at me with a pensive frown. "I've found these bones."

I look down at the skeletal bones scattered in the dust.

"I know," I say, feeling a prickle of fear creep across my skin. "Horrible, isn't it? Adjoa says they were sacrificed."

Ibrahim nods. "And it looks like they did something to them too." He picks up one of the scattered bones and shows it to me. "Look."

The bone that he's holding looks like a femur – the long bone you find in the upper leg. This one is about half a metre long, but as Ibrahim turns the bone over I see there's something strange about it. One end of the bone is rounded like normal, but the other end seems to have been sharpened to a chisel edge.

"Is it a weapon, do you think?"

Taking it from his hand, I stare at the sharpened bone, trying to work out what it might have been used for. I don't think it's a weapon – it's not a spear or a sword, even though its edge looks sharp enough to cut. Strangely the shape of it reminds me more of a doorstop, one of those things that you wedge under the bottom of a door to stop it from banging shut. Although here, there's no door to hold open...

I look up to meet Ibrahim's gaze. His head is tilted slightly to one side as if he's looking at the world from a different angle. I remember what Adjoa called him as we walked through the stacks in the library. She said he was a *finder* – someone who sees the things everyone else has missed. This bone must be important somehow.

I hear the sound of a hand slapped against stone and look back to see Oscar and Adjoa still arguing across the sarcophagus lid.

"If we can't lift it, then we'll just have to break it

open," Oscar growls.

Adjoa was right. Oscar's a destroyer.

But as I look from the flagstone lid that rests on top of the sarcophagus to the chiselled bone that I'm holding, an idea slides into the front of my mind. Maybe this puzzle needs brains rather than brute force, after all...

Clambering to my feet, I head back to Oscar and Adjoa. As the two of them bicker, I peer instead at the edge of the sarcophagus, where the heavy lid meets the stone coffin beneath. It's almost a perfect seal, but in a couple of places I see cracks and slivers where the stone has been chipped away. They're only knife-thin, but if my idea is going to work, I hope this will do the trick.

Carefully lining up the bone, I place its sharp chisel edge against one of the cracks.

"What are you doing?" Oscar asks, casting a dismissive glance in my direction.

"Lifting the lid," I reply.

"On your own? With a bone?" Oscar laughs out loud. "You've got no chance."

"It's not a bone, it's a lever," I tell him, sliding the chiselled edge between the base and the lid of the sarcophagus. "And with the right lever you can move the whole world."

With all the strength I can muster I pull down hard on the rounded end of the bone.

The lid starts to lift, only millimetres at first, but as I strain to force the lever down, the gap starts to widen, the flagstone lid suddenly sliding away with a rumbling sound before crashing to the floor with a deafening boom.

Oscar jumps back with a yelp of surprise.

Breathing hard, I stand stock-still for a second, still holding the sharpened bone. It actually worked. But there's no time to catch my breath as the others quickly crowd round the now open sarcophagus.

"You did it," Adjoa says, reaching out to squeeze my hand as I join her there. "That was incredible, Ami! Now we can find out what the Answer is."

Oscar lets out a low whistle as he peers inside the sarcophagus. "Who cares what the Answer is," he says. "It looks like we've found ourselves some proper treasure here."

A skeleton lies on its back inside the sarcophagus, its bones perfectly preserved. Surrounding it I can see countless pieces of exquisite jewellery: jade necklaces, silver bracelets and golden rings. Beads of malachite and pearl lie scattered among tiny carved figurines, but it's not the sight of this treasure that makes me gasp. It's the layer of bright-red dust that covers it all.

"I'm having this," Oscar says, reaching for a crown that rests on top of the crimson skull. But before he can grab it, Adjoa knocks his hand away.

"Don't touch it!" she shouts, her voice thick with fear. "That red dust is cinnabar."

"So what?" Oscar says, turning angrily towards her. "This stuff's worth a fortune – a bit of cinnamon isn't going to do me any harm."

"Not cinnamon," Adjoa replies, standing her ground as Oscar tries to stare her down. "*Cinnabar.* It means 'dragon's blood' and it's the most toxic mineral on Earth. Just one touch can kill you." The flickering light cast by the torch makes her eyes shine. "It's the perfect booby trap."

Oscar takes a step back from the dust-encrusted crown, but Ibrahim is still peering inside the sarcophagus.

"Who do you think this is?" he asks.

Adjoa looks down at the crimson skeleton. "It's the Red Queen of Palenque," she says, keeping her voice low as if she's afraid of waking the dead. "A Mayan noblewoman whose tomb was found in the thirteenth temple of a lost city, deep in the jungles of Mexico. Nobody knows her true identity, but the treasures she was buried with led some to believe she was the last Mayan queen. Her body was painted with this dust because it was the same colour as the rising sun and the Mayans thought it would give her the power to rise as well. The Red Queen would live again."

I shiver at the thought of this, then glance back over my shoulder at the rest of the bones, scattered among our footprints in the dust. No chance of a new life for any of those. Maybe the people with the treasure are the only ones that matter…

"I thought you said we'd find the Answer in here," Oscar growls, still looking annoyed by the fact that he can't get his hands on these riches. "What was the point of opening the lid if it doesn't take us anywhere? There's no gateway here, just a pile of dusty old bones."

Adjoa frowns, but this time she's got no reply. I look again at the crimson skeleton, every piece of treasure caked in the poisonous dust. Maybe Oscar's right. Maybe this is just a red herring…

But as my gaze roams across the riches draped over the Red Queen's bones, I glimpse something that seems out of place. Fine pieces of jewellery shine beneath the dust, but between her skeletal fingers the Red Queen seems to be holding a simple seashell.

Inside my mind I hear the Host's words. *The Answer might be found in the most unexpected of places.*

Pulling a handkerchief from my pocket, I use it to cover my hand and then reach inside the sarcophagus.

"Careful, Ami," Adjoa breathes as I ease the seashell from the Red Queen's grasp. "Don't touch the dust."

The outside of the seashell is painted copper-red, but as I turn it over carefully in my hand, I see a stone carving hidden inside the shell. It's shaped like a butterfly, its wings marked with the same pattern as the lid. There's no dust inside the shell, so I carefully pick the carved object out with my free hand, before dropping the shell and the handkerchief back into the open coffin.

As I stare down at the stone butterfly, the others crowd round to take a closer look.

"What is it?" Oscar asks.

"I'm not sure," I reply, holding the tiny sculpture to the light.

As the torchlight flickers, striped patterns of gold shimmer across the butterfly's wings. I know it's only a trick of the light, but it looks like it's about to take flight.

"It's the Galactic Butterfly," Adjoa says, the ghost of a smile creeping across her lips. "The Hunab Ku."

As she says this, I feel excitement spark inside my chest. Adjoa said before that the Hunab Ku showed the gateway to all knowledge. I glance around at the stone walls that surround us, at the gods and monsters guarding this place. This butterfly seems to be carved from the same stone, almost like it should fit somewhere here. And as I stare at the strange hieroglyphs that mark the end wall of the chamber, something seems to click inside my mind.

"If we're looking for the Answer, maybe this is the key."

Still holding the stone butterfly, I walk towards the far wall, my gaze searching for what I know must be there.

"What are you looking for?" Ibrahim asks, hurrying to join me.

My fingers trace the shapes of the hieroglyphs,

the patterns they make swirling in spirals across the solid stone. The graven faces of jaguars and alligators stare sightlessly back at me, their teeth bared in snarls as if I'm trespassing.

"A way out," I tell him, still searching for a place where the carving might fit. "That's what we've been looking for all along. The hatch in the attic, the door in the library – this game is called The Escape, so that's what must be hidden here: some kind of gate that will let us escape." I glance down at the stone butterfly. "And I think this is the key we need to open it."

I look back at the wall, peering into its shadowy cracks and crevices. As well as the strange faces of beasts and men, I can see the shapes of seashells, circles and lines sculpted out of the stone.

"What do you think they mean?" Ibrahim asks, his gaze following mine as we trace the spiralling shapes of the hieroglyphs. But before I can answer, Adjoa jumps in with her reply.

"I think they tell the time," she says, suddenly appearing right by my side.

Behind us, I hear a sniggering laugh.

"You mean like a clock?" Oscar says, swaggering up to join us as we scour the wall for clues. "Well, it looks like it's stopped."

I know he's trying to be funny, but as I stare at the circular patterns that the hieroglyphs make, I can't help but think that it *does* look like a giant clock face.

"It's not a clock," Adjoa replies, reaching up towards the outermost circle where midnight would strike. "It's a calendar." She starts to trace the shape of this circle, passing over each of the carved hieroglyphs as they spiral round. "The Mayans didn't just have one calendar like people do today but three. This is the Haab, a solar calendar that lasts for 365 days. Each of these symbols is a Mayan month – *Zotz*, *Tzec*, *Xul*, *Yaxkin* and more – eighteen months that each lasted for twenty days." As her hand sweeps round to near the start of the circle again, Adjoa pauses, her fingers hovering over a strange hieroglyph that looks like a scream. "And a nineteenth month of five nameless days that the Mayans called the *Wayeb*. This was a time of great danger when the Mayans believed the gates to the underworld were opened and chaos unleashed on the world."

Adjoa's hushed words echo off the walls of the tomb and I feel my skin prickle with fear. We might be looking for a gate, but as I stare at these carved jaws, I just hope it isn't the one to the underworld.

Moving her hand Adjoa starts to trace a second circle of hieroglyphs, a wheel within a wheel spiralling round.

"This is the Tzolkin," she says. "It's the calendar the Mayans used to mark their sacred days. Feasts, festivals and ceremonies – all were determined by the Tzolkin. The Mayans believed it could even predict the future."

Mesmerised, I watch as Adjoa's fingers follow the hieroglyphs round, shadows falling across these eerie carvings.

"The Mayans didn't see time as a straight line," she explains, "but as a circle turning round. History repeats itself – what has happened before will happen again. The Mayans believed that time was an endlessly turning cycle that went on and on."

"Just like you," Oscar mutters under his breath.

Adjoa ignores him, her fingers coming to rest in the centre of the circle.

"Until the end of the Long Count," she says. "This is the calendar the Mayans used to count the days since the world was created. An age they believed would last for two million, eight hundred and eighty thousand days."

Adjoa moves her hand away from the wall and I see the cluster of hieroglyphs that mark the Long Count. The sculpted shapes of monstrous faces leer back at me, skull-like birds and jaguars, but nestled in the centre of them I see the shadow of a hollow in the stone. Peering closer, I see that this tiny cavity has been carved in the shape of a butterfly and, as I compare it to the stone I'm holding, I realise it's a perfect match.

"This is it," I say, noticing a faint red glow that seems to emanate from deep inside the hollow. "I think I've found the keyhole."

13

I hold the stone butterfly between my fingertips, the spiral patterns on its wings lit with an eerie red glow. It looks as though it's been carved from this hollow, the red light that gleams coming from deep inside. It's the same light that I've seen all the way through this game – the one that's telling me now that I must be right.

As the others crowd round my shoulders, I carefully place the butterfly inside the keyhole, feeling the carving click into place.

"It fits," Adjoa whispers, her voice hushed in the shadows.

Holding my breath, I wait to see what happens next, but as the seconds stretch into silence I'm forced to let it out again in a puzzled sigh.

"This can't be right," I say, peering closer to see a faint glow still glimmering round the edge of the butterfly's wings. "It hasn't worked."

"It *has* to work," Adjoa says. "It all fits – the gateway, the butterfly, the Hunab Ku. This has to be the key."

I turn round, looking to the others for any kind of clue. Ibrahim frowns, his fingers fidgeting as if the hieroglyphs are a Rubik's cube for him to solve. Oscar has his arms folded nonchalantly across his chest and a know-it-all look on his face.

"What is it?" I snap, his smirk already annoying me.

"If you think it's a key," Oscar says, speaking slowly as if I'm stupid, "don't you need to turn it?"

I blink. He's right.

Turning back to the wall, I reach for the butterfly. The carved stone feels smooth, but as I start to turn it, I hear a juddering sound like the grinding of ancient gears. The spiralling hieroglyphs suddenly shine with an eerie red light and I watch as the wheels start to turn.

"It's working," Adjoa says, a buzz of excitement in her voice. "Keep turning."

As I slowly twist the stone butterfly, the hieroglyphs continue to revolve. Mesmerised, I watch as the snarling stone faces wheel round, the roar of hidden machinery making the wall shake. As it turns, the outer wheel seems to be counting the months off, the symbols that Adjoa showed us glowing red as each one glides by, while the inner wheel seems to turn back time as it revolves anti-clockwise. I keep on turning the key, waiting for a click that never comes.

"I don't understand," I say, raising my voice over the clattering noise. "If this is the gate, why won't it open? What else do we need to do?"

"Let me try," Oscar says, pushing me out of the way to get his hand on the key. "There's a knack to these things."

But as he twists the butterfly key, the concentric rings of hieroglyphs just keep turning, the tomb shaking as they revolve in opposite directions. I glance up in fear as shards of stone start to fall from the ceiling. If we don't stop turning the wheels, we're going to be buried alive. A crimson glow seems to seep through the carved symbols and faces, the colour blood-red, but there's no sign of any gate starting to open.

"Maybe it's not a gate," Ibrahim says, almost as if he's reading my mind. "Maybe this is more like the door to a safe that's keeping the Answer locked away. The only way to open it is to find the right combination."

I look across at Ibrahim, his head tilted to one side as he watches the hieroglyphs turn.

"This isn't just a calendar, it's a time lock," he says.

As his words sink in, the revolving symbols seem to sharpen into view. It's like my brain is tuning out all the noise and distractions to focus on the one thing that matters. It's not tunnel vision – it's puzzle vision. And if Ibrahim's right, the hieroglyphs are hiding the Answer. I turn towards Adjoa, her brow furrowed as she watches the wheels turn. "We need to find the right date to open the gate."

She nods in reply, her gaze fixed on the turning wheels as rocks tumble from the ceiling of the tomb.

"The Long Count lasts for two million, eight hundred and eighty thousand days. That's nearly eight thousand years. We can't try out every date in the hope of finding the right one by accident, but there's one date that made the Mayans famous. The twenty-first of December 2012 – the day the Long Count said the world would come to an end."

She turns towards me, her dark eyes shining in the flickering torchlight.

"That's got to be the date that'll open the gate – the date that will give us the Answer and bring this game to an end."

I glance up at the stone carvings as the wheels in the wall continue to turn. The eerie red light that seems to seep through every hieroglyph glows brightest as they reach the highest point before fading a little as they slip from the zenith. This must be the place where the date is marked, but as I stare at the spiralling stones I can't tell which of the symbols show the end of the Long Count.

Adjoa, though, looks like she can. Elbowing Oscar out of the way, she grabs hold of the key and, gritting her teeth, starts to turn it more quickly. As the hieroglyphs whirl round with a clattering roar, Adjoa keeps her gaze fixed on the highest point of the wheel, watching as each carved face briefly blazes crimson-red before moving on to the next. Then she breathes a single word out loud. "Now."

With a squealing, grating roar the stone wheels

judder to a halt as Adjoa stops turning the key. As rocks fall from the roof of the tomb, she points towards the hieroglyphs that shine the brightest.

"That's the end of the thirteenth *baktun*," she says, gesturing towards a sinister face halfway up the wall. "The last day of the Long Count. It has to be the right date."

As I stare up at the stony profile, its single eye gleams red. Two more hieroglyphs are set directly above it and I see, with a shudder, that the highest of these shows a skeletal jaw.

There's a second of silence and then, directly behind me, I hear a scraping noise, like the sound of bone scratching against stone.

Turning round with a mounting sense of dread, I see the Red Queen slowly rising from her tomb.

14

"Get back!" Adjoa shouts, scrambling to escape as the crimson skeleton staggers towards us. "Don't let her touch you!"

Swathes of cinnabar dust fall from the Red Queen's fingers as she reaches out a skeletal claw. A jade crown hangs skewed atop her skull, teeth bared in a ghostlike grin as a red light gleams from eyeless sockets. Frozen in fear, I can't pull myself away, my gaze locked on hers as the tomb shakes with a rumbling roar.

Oscar hammers on the wall, the solid stone refusing to shift. "Let us out! Let us out!" he yells.

But the Host isn't listening. The Red Queen rules this place now.

Behind her, the shapes of more skeletal figures are slowly picking themselves up from the floor, the bones of the Mayan dead rising again to serve their queen. I glance back at the wheels of hieroglyphs, trying to work out how we got everything so wrong.

At the highest point of the motionless wheels I see a stone-carved scream. The skeletal jaws of the hieroglyph gape wide like an open gate. I remember the name that Adjoa gave to this symbol – the *Wayeb* – the dangerous month of nameless days when the Mayans believed the gates to the underworld were opened. That's what we've done now – we've opened the gates to Hell.

I hear a sudden hiss and I spin round to see the Red Queen standing right in front of me, her skeletal arms spread wide. As she lunges to wrap me in a deadly embrace, Adjoa drags me clear, the two of us stumbling backwards as rocks tumble down. Slipping on broken stone, I feel my ankle twist and can't stop myself from falling to the floor.

Lifting my head, I see the Red Queen turning

towards Ibrahim. He's standing in front of the spiralling hieroglyphs, his head bent as he inspects the stone butterfly that lies at its heart. He doesn't even seem to notice she's there, lost in thought as his fingers fidget and twitch in search of the Answer.

I open my mouth wide, ready to call out a warning, but then I catch sight of something crawling on the ground. It's not much bigger than a grain of rice, its spiky-black body bristling as it wriggles forward in a wavelike motion.

It's a caterpillar.

The tiny creature is treading a perfect circle in the dust in front of my eyes. Its segmented body writhes as it winds its way round, the sight of this strangely mesmerising. Inside my head I hear the Host mocking me.

Look around carefully. Everything is part of the game.

This must *mean* something.

My mind races as I remember what Adjoa told me about the Mayans. How they thought time was an endlessly turning circle. I watch the caterpillar trace the same shape in the dust. I think about what I know about these tiny creatures, racking my brain for any kind of clue. How the caterpillar only lives for a couple of weeks. How they eat and eat and eat…

"Ibrahim!"

I hear Adjoa's anguished scream, but my gaze stays fixed on the circling caterpillar. Then I hear a whisper inside my head, Min's voice reminding me what comes next.

I dreamed I was a butterfly.

With a dawning realisation I look up at the solid-stone wall. The wheels of hieroglyphs stand motionless, but as my eyes follow the spiralling shapes that they make, I realise the circle has no end. The end is the beginning too. The caterpillar becomes a butterfly…

My thoughts crystallise into cold, hard certainty. What I need to do now is suddenly very clear.

I scramble to my feet, heading straight for the centre of the spiralling hieroglyphs. Close by, Adjoa looks on aghast as the Red Queen sways like a bone marionette, turning to face Oscar as he backs into a corner of the tomb.

"Come on," he shouts, his eyes blazing with fury. "I'm not scared of you and your stupid army."

In reply to his shout I hear the scrape of bone against stone again as the Red Queen and her servants prepare to strike. This is my chance – the split-second distraction I needed to grab hold of the butterfly key. The stone feels warm beneath my fingertips, the shape of the wings spread in perfect symmetry as I give the key one final twist.

There's a click and then the stone wheels start turning once more, trundling on to the next hieroglyph before stopping again with a shudder. The stone butterfly slips from my fingers, retracting into the hollow as I stagger back in surprise.

"Ami," Adjoa calls out, her voice echoing off the shaking walls. "What have you done?"

I see a glint of gold at the heart of the hollow and watch as it starts to grow.

"I've changed the date," I reply as the golden gleam seems to flutter more brightly. There's something moving inside the widening hole. "It wasn't the last day of the Long Count that we needed, but the first day of the next. The circle keeps on turning. We can only find the Answer if we start again."

The hollow has now grown to the size of a small window and it's getting bigger with every passing second. The hieroglyphs at the centre of the stones start to crumble away, revealing the golden wings of countless butterflies. These start to stream through the opening gate, the butterflies pouring forth in a never-ending torrent.

The Red Queen screams as the butterflies swarm around her, her crimson bones disappearing beneath a beating tide of golden wings.

"This way!" I shout, calling out to Adjoa and Oscar as the tomb continues to shake. I can't see Ibrahim anywhere, just the skeletal bones of the Red Queen's servants flailing against the oncoming storm as the butterflies continue to swarm.

I hold my arm out in front of me, groping my way through this golden haze of beating wings. Oscar's already at the gate, clambering through as Adjoa appears by my side.

"Where's Ibrahim?" I shout, raising my voice above the beating thunder.

"It's too late, Ami," she moans, tears streaming down her face. "We've got to get out of this place."

She grabs hold of my arm and starts pulling me through the gate; the relentless tide of butterflies is still streaming through. Beyond their golden wings, I glimpse blackness ahead and the faint outline of metallic steps climbing down in the dark.

As Adjoa drags me with her and Oscar steams down the steps, there's nothing else I can do but follow them.

15

The metallic stairs ring with the sound of our footsteps as we descend. I can see the outlines of Adjoa and Oscar ahead of me in the gloom, all of us walking now in single file as the handrails on either side guide us down in parallel lines.

I've stopped asking Adjoa what happened to Ibrahim in the tomb; her tearful replies only tell me that he's gone. Just like Min. This game is picking us off one by one.

There's a spreading brightness up ahead, the stairs getting shallower with every tread that I take. I can see now that we're climbing down a ruined escalator, its frozen steps carpeted with broken shards of glass that crunch beneath my trainers.

It looks like we're entering some kind of shopping mall. A huge clock hangs on the far side of a soaring atrium, the brightness coming from the skylights that cover its domed ceiling. Through these airy windows I can see a distant blue, but as the hands of the clock stand at twelve minutes past eight, I can't really tell whether it's a.m. or p.m.

Oscar's the first to reach the final stair, his striding steps taking him across the empty concourse. I look around as I join Adjoa there and take in a scene of utter destruction. Piles of debris litter the wide-open space: shattered glass and ripped-out shelving, smashed display cabinets and broken plant pots. Near the centre of the atrium, a drained fountain is filled with dust, while withered plants scatter trails of dead leaves across the tiles.

It looks like this place has been abandoned for years.

Oscar's still striding ahead, his echoing steps taking him past a deserted customer service desk.

"Where are you going?" I call out after him. "We've got to stick together, especially now."

Oscar stops in his tracks, turning towards me

with a look of contempt.

"Why?" he replies, his shout causing a flock of wild pigeons to take flight from their hidden perches. As they soar towards the skylights, their slate-grey wings flecked with bronze, Oscar rounds on me. "Why do we have to stick together? It's not done us any good so far, has it? Take a look around, Ami. We're not the Five Mind or the Awesome Foursome. There's just the three of us now. We're not a team, full stop – we're competitors. And I'm going to make sure I find the Answer first."

Oscar turns to leave, tossing a final comment over his shoulder. "And don't even think about following me."

I stand there, speechless, and watch him go. The path he takes through the piles of broken things leads towards an arcade of shops. It's darker over there away from the atrium's skylights, but I can just make out the sight of shuttered storefronts.

"Let him go," Adjoa says, walking instead towards the customer service desk. "We don't need him either."

I look around the deserted mall, more galleries of shops branching off to the left and right. These faded arcades are plunged into darkness too and, as

I strain my eyes against the shadows, the ghost of a shiver runs down my spine. This place should be filled with light and life. I'm not scared of the dark, but I can't stop myself from wondering what it's hiding. It's the fear of the unknown.

"Ami!" Adjoa's excited shout makes me turn. She's standing by the customer service desk, holding up a crumpled piece of paper. "Come and see what I've found."

Hurrying over, I take the scrap of paper from her, feeling puzzled as I read the words written there.

GOLDEN
FROZEN
JUMPER
HUNTER
EX I T

I look up at Adjoa and see a glint of delight sparkling in her eyes.

"What is it?" I ask, struggling to work out why she's so excited. The words don't make any sense at all.

"Isn't it obvious?" Adjoa replies with a grin. "It's a shopping list."

I look again at the list, turning each word over in my mind: golden, frozen, jumper, hunter, exit. I shake my head. If this is a shopping list, I don't know what it wants us to buy. Seeing my frown, Adjoa starts to explain.

"Remember what the Host said," she says, the toes of her neon-green trainers tapping out a fidgety rhythm on the floor. "Everything is part of the game. This list was left here, waiting for us. This must be a scavenger hunt."

"A scavenger hunt?"

"One of those games where you get a list of things to find. Some people call them treasure hunts, but the winner's always the one who's the first to get every single item on the list. That must be what this is – a list of the things we need to find the Answer."

She takes the list, turning again to face the customer service desk. The front edge slopes towards us, displaying a store directory and map of the shopping mall. On it I can see the arcades branching off in three directions from this central atrium, the galleries of shops marked out in red, green and blue.

"This is our chance, Ami," Adjoa says as she inspects the colour-coded map. "If we want to beat

Oscar to the Answer, we just have to follow this plan."

I glance down at the store directory. I didn't think our mission to save the world would end with a shopping trip, but what Adjoa's saying kind of makes sense. Since we started playing The Escape we've been trying to find the Answer, but nobody said it was just one thing. Maybe this list tells us the ingredients we need to *create* the Answer. And if she's right, this means we've got a head start on Oscar.

"So where do we go first?" I ask, trailing my finger down the list of shops, arranged by category. "Beauty and Fragrances? Books, Cards and Stationery? Electronics? Entertainment? Fashion?"

Adjoa shakes her head, pointing instead to a heading halfway down the list.

"Jewellery," she replies with a confident smile. "The list says the first thing we're looking for is golden, so we're bound to find something there. A gold ring or a necklace maybe – anything like that."

Her finger moves across to point out the store's location on the map, halfway along the left-hand gallery.

"After that we'll head to a food store to find something frozen," she continues, plotting out the route that we'll take, "before moving on to fashion to grab ourselves a jumper." Glancing up, Adjoa flashes me a grin. "We're going to finish this game in style."

I try to force a smile but something's still troubling me.

"What about the other things?" I ask, reaching out to take the list from Adjoa again. "Where are we going to find a hunter?"

"We don't need to find a hunter," she replies. "We *are* the hunters and once we get the things on the list we'll find the Answer too. It's all we need to finish the game and get out of this place. That's what 'EXIT' means – the end is in sight, Ami."

I look up to meet my friend's gaze. Even though she's smiling, Adjoa's eyes look hollowed out, the tears she cried before leaving dark circles behind.

I think about Ibrahim and Min and everything that we've seen so far. The burning attic and the library of dust, the cursed tomb and now this deserted shopping mall. And as I think, I can't stop myself from asking the question out loud.

"Do you still think it's a game?"

Adjoa bites her lip, almost as if she's afraid to reply.

"It has to be," she says finally. "And we need to make sure that we win it."

Adjoa turns to head for the darkened arcade, starting to follow the same route that her finger drew. Glancing back over her shoulder, she beckons me on. "Come on, Ami."

16

"What do you think happened here?" I ask, peering into the shifting shadows as we make our way along the darkened arcade. Broken glass crunches underfoot as we pass by the shuttered storefronts, their empty facades dented and torn. We've got no torch to light our path, so instead have to rely on the shafts of light that fall from cracked ceiling tiles, these faint patches of brightness illuminating the puddles and piles of debris that populate this place instead of people. "Where is everybody?"

"I don't know," Adjoa replies, her voice close to me in the dark. "But at least we don't have to worry about queuing for the sales."

I shiver as I spot a headless mannequin lying in the dust, the sight reminding me of the piles of bones in the Red Queen's tomb. REDUCED signs are strewn around the shop dummy, their labels proudly proclaiming that EVERYTHING MUST GO. But as I listen to the silence that fills the shopping mall, it looks like everything already has.

Everything's gone.

A wave of sadness crashes over me. Dad said the game was going to be the perfect gift, but all I've found inside The Escape is senseless destruction. This can't be what he meant for me. The only thing I've got left to cling to now is the hope that the Answer might make sense of everything. If we can find it…

"I think this is it," Adjoa says, interrupting my thoughts with a tug on my arm.

She's come to a halt in front of another faceless store, the name of the shop above the shutters peeled away, leaving only the last letters behind.

ELLERS

Just like all the other stores that we've passed, this jewellers lies in darkness. Slatted metal shutters are pulled down in front of the store, but it looks like someone has taken an axe to them. A huge jagged hole has been torn in the metal, its sharp edges curling outwards to show the way in.

"Follow me."

Taking the lead, Adjoa steps through shards of glass to squeeze through the gap in the shutters.

"Are you sure we should be doing this?" I ask as I follow her through, a nervous feeling gnawing at my insides.

Adjoa doesn't answer straight away; her trainers crunch through broken glass as her silhouette is suddenly outlined with a strange blue light. "Look at this."

Somehow it's lighter inside the store, due to a luminescent glow that seems to rise from the ground. I look around, my brain struggling to make sense of what I can see. It's like I'm looking at an underwater scene, the shattered glass that carpets the floor glinting with an iridescent light. It looks like a sea of shining things glimmering blue-green. At first I think they're the sparkling shapes of fish, but then I realise they're watches, their luminous faces and ticking hands glistening in the dark.

As my eyes adjust, I start to make out the smashed display cases, the glass cabinets shattered with their contents strewn across the floor. Amid the luminous watch dials, I can see the silvery trails of earrings and necklaces, sparkling like treasure on the ocean bed.

"I didn't think it would be this easy," Adjoa says, squatting close to the ground as she starts to search through the scattered jewellery. "There's got to be something golden here."

I'm about to start looking too when I hear a sound, soft padding footsteps that seem to be coming from the back of the store. I turn round, thinking this must be Oscar on the trail of the Answer too, and then I see it.

Built like a bear, it stands just as tall as it prowls forward on four powerful legs. Its golden fur shines in the glimmering half-light as it pads towards me. I hold my breath, unable to believe what I'm seeing as I stare into the eyes of the biggest cat I've ever seen. These shine golden too, but it's the two long sharp teeth that curve down from its upper jaw that make my heart thump in fear.

It's a sabre-toothed tiger.

"Now this is pretty," Adjoa says, holding up a glittering necklace. "But I think it's platinum, not gold."

She hasn't seen it yet, her gaze still fixed on the trinkets scattered across the floor.

I want to shout out – to warn Adjoa what's happening – but the words die on my lips as I watch the tiger open its jaws wide. We came here looking for something golden but I think it's found us instead.

And then the sabre-toothed tiger pounces, springing forward with a guttural roar.

Time seems to slow to a crawl as I throw myself backwards, my vision filled with teeth and claws. Their blades swipe the air where I was standing only moments before as the tiger lands with a snarl of frustration, its powerful claws grinding the shards of glass into dust.

"What the—"

Adjoa turns, her eyes opening wide in fear as she sees the extinct animal clawing the ground only metres away. Grabbing hold of her, I scramble for the exit, the sabre-toothed tiger snarling at our heels. As we squeeze through the gap ripped in the shutters, the metal judders as the hulking creature slams its body against the slats.

I turn round, gripping the jagged metal edges as I try to push them closed to stop the creature coming through. The shutters shake as the sabre-tooth slams itself against them again; the metal groans as if the whole thing is going to come down.

"What is that thing?" Adjoa gasps, her voice frantic in my ear.

Gritting my teeth against the pain, I force the sharp edges together; the shutters shake again with a hideous scratching as the beast claws at the closing gap. It's impossible to know how long this will hold it for, but then it's impossible to think it's even here. The sabre-toothed tiger died out thousands of years ago.

We've got to get out of here. I turn round, staring into the shadows as I try to remember the way back. The darkened arcade looks different now, the hulking shapes of frozen statues looming in the gloom. The largest looks as big as an elephant, its shadowy bulk practically touching the ceiling as it blocks the path ahead.

Adjoa screams as the sabre-tooth slams its body against the shutters again. The metal judders, dislodging tiles from the ceiling. As they fall, fresh shafts of light shine on the scene, illuminating the hulking shadow straight ahead.

What I thought was a statue is actually an animal, its colossal frame covered in a coat of thick reddish-brown hair. It stands on legs as thick as tree trunks, its broad sloping back rising to a peaked dome. I hear its coarse hair rustling as its massive head turns towards me and then I see its long curved tusks, the shape of these silhouetted like twin question marks in the half-light.

I blink – not just my eyes, but my brain too – unable to process what I can see right in front of me. And then the beast raises its trunk as it lets out a trumpeting call that shakes the entire mall.

It's a woolly mammoth.

17

I stand there frozen, staring up at a creature that shouldn't exist.

Its ivory trunks curve sharply towards me, their length maybe three metres or more. Small woolly ears flank the sides of its strange domed head, its dark eyes staring straight into mine. Then the metal shutters behind us rattle again violently with the snarling rage of the sabre-tooth still caged inside.

The mammoth's trunk flies up into the air, blaring out another siren note of warning. I see the shadows of other things behind it in the darkness start to move and then I realise they're heading straight for us.

"Run!" Adjoa shouts, grabbing hold of my arm as the mammoth begins its stampeding charge. The ground shakes as we stumble towards the shelter of a sweetshop stand. Ripped-out seats are piled up against this candy-coloured stall and we cower behind them, crouching in fear as, over the sound of thunder, we hear a deafening chorus of trumpeting calls.

I watch open-mouthed as the shadowy herd of woolly mammoths crashes past our hiding place, their trunks lashing from side to side as they stampede. Lurching in panic, one of the frantic beasts slams against the darkened front of the jewellery store, its curling tusks tearing the shutters away.

As the mammoth reels, I hear the triumphant roar of the now-freed sabre-toothed tiger. The sound of the stampede is slowly receding, but as the mammoth moves forward again with a shake of its head, I watch as a golden shadow starts to stalk its lumbering steps.

"What do we do now?" Adjoa whispers, her body pressed close to mine as we shelter behind our makeshift hide.

Raising my finger to my lips, I silently gesture for her to follow me as I start to creep in the opposite direction. In the distance I hear the mammoths trumpeting and hope that the sabre-toothed tiger is still on their trail, not ours.

The wide walkway that leads through the arcade of shops still lies in darkness, but as I step between the shadows, I think I can see more shapes in the dark. It's impossible to make out any details, the faint shafts of light that glimmer in places illuminating only silhouettes. But these pitch-black shadows are moving, the bulky shapes of animals emerging from obscurity. I can see bears and bison, giant deer with antlers so large they seem to span the entire gallery. I think I can see something that looks like a rhino but covered in a coat of thick, shaggy hair. And there are even stranger animals that I don't recognise with sweeping horns and huge terrifying beaks.

I freeze. There's no way through this shadowy menagerie and, as I hear the thundering tread of the mammoths behind us, no way back either. I glance around, looking for any way out.

Most of the stores lie in darkness, their shutters rolled down against the storm, but then I glimpse a faint crack of light from one of the shopfronts. Unlike the other shops, there are no shutters here.

The front of this store is boarded with hoardings instead. In the semi-darkness I can just read the words "RENOVATION WORK IN PROGRESS" written across the front of them.

The light is coming from a crack in a hoarding, a sliver of silver showing the way in. Or maybe it's a way out.

"This way," I whisper, tugging at Adjoa's arm.

Moving as quietly as we can, we hurry towards the boarded-up store. Peeling back the broken hoarding, I hold it open for Adjoa to clamber through and wince as the silvery light spills out across the arcade. Glancing back fearfully over my shoulder to check that none of the shadowy beasts have spotted us, I quickly follow her through, letting the heavy board swing back into place.

It's even brighter inside the store and I blink as my eyes take a moment to adjust to the light. It's coming from a safety lamp that's positioned near the entrance, the full glare of its beam angled towards the store's interior. There I can see empty shelving units and clothes rails arranged in rows across a tiled floor. Half of these look like they're ready for ripping out, the yellowing shelves cracked and broken, while others look brand new, standing shrink-wrapped in clear plastic film. Electric cables hang in places from the ceiling, their bare wires twined together like withered vines.

"What do we do now?" Adjoa says, keeping her voice low as we step further inside the store. "Those things out there…"

Her words trail away as we hear a scampering tread coming from the first aisle of shelving. Adjoa's hand grabs for mine, her fingernails digging into my skin. Inside my head, I see the golden sabre-tooth, its teeth and claws coming straight for me.

The sound comes again; its hiccuping rhythm making my heart leap. I wait for the creature to reveal itself as Adjoa moans in fear. Then the scampering stops and I see a tiny furry face peering round the end of the shelving unit.

I can't help but laugh as the creature hops round the corner, my worst fears dissolving in front of my eyes.

It's a baby kangaroo.

Shaking off Adjoa's hand, I crouch down as the joey hops towards me on scampering paws. Its ash-brown pelt fades to grey as it reaches the end of its tail, while the fur on its belly is a soft sandy colour. Standing upright, the baby kangaroo reaches only halfway to my knee, but as I stare into its eyes, shining like black pearls, I can't help feel that it's judging me.

"Hey," I say, keeping my voice gentle so as not to scare it.

The baby kangaroo chirps in reply. Then it hops up on to my lap and starts nestling itself in the crook of my arm.

"You shouldn't pick it up," Adjoa says, a note of warning in her voice. "It's a wild animal."

"Shhhhhh." I stroke the joey with my free hand, feeling the warmth of its soft, silky fur. "You'll scare it."

The kangaroo peers up at me inquisitively. There's a distinctive black mark on its face that reaches in a V from its nose to its eyes, while the lighter fur below is a buff-yellow colour.

"Where have you come from?" I wonder out loud.

"I'm more worried about the rest of them," Adjoa replies, stealing a glance back towards the hoardings. "We still need to get out of here, Ami."

I nod my head and then frown as my hand snags on a strange square of material halfway down the joey's back.

"What's this?"

It looks like a label and the kangaroo wriggles as I try to look more closely at it.

"Stay still," I tell it, trying to soothe the squirming animal as my fingers gently investigate the label that seems to be stitched into its fur. Slowly, this seems to do the trick and the joey's ears prick up inquisitively as I start to read the writing on the label out loud.

"*The toolache wallaby, pronounced* too-late-shee, *was a native of Australia. The most elegant, graceful and swift member of the kangaroo family, the toolache wallaby was hunted to extinction by man. The last toolache lived for twelve years in captivity and died in 1939...*"

My voice trails away as the wallaby looks up at me with bright eyes. I can't believe anyone would want to hurt something so beautiful. Nuzzling against my skin, the toolache makes a soft chirping sound as if it's trying to tell me something.

"It's OK," I say, still stroking its ash-brown fur. I can feel the warmth of its body next to mine. It feels so alive, but this label stitched into its fur makes it seem like a toy. "I'll keep you safe, Tooey."

The wallaby chirrups again, echoing the sound of its name.

Tchoo-ey.

"That's right," I say. "I'm going to call you Tooey."

I smile as I glance up at Adjoa, but my friend's face is still furrowed in a frown.

"What's the matter?" I ask her. "Don't you think she looks like a Tooey?"

"It's not her name that's the matter, Ami," Adjoa replies, her freckles crinkling with worry lines. "It's the fact she's even here."

"What do you mean?"

"Think about everything we've seen since we arrived inside this mall," Adjoa says, her anxious words worming their way inside my brain. "The sabre-toothed tiger, the woolly mammoths, all those impossible creatures outside. Even this baby kangaroo—"

"It's a wallaby," I say, still snuggling the creature close to me.

"It's not supposed to be here, Ami!" Adjoa snaps, the sharp sound of her voice making Tooey squirm in my lap. "None of these animals should be. They all died out years ago."

Still squatting, I shift uncomfortably as my brain ticks off the words from the list one by one.

GOLDEN
FROZEN
JUMPER

A sudden clatter makes me turn towards the boarded-up entrance, Tooey burrowing into my arms. Adjoa spins round, picking up a metal pole. Brandishing this like a weapon, she stands ready to defend us as we watch something push its way through the broken hoarding.

The safety lamp is aimed straight towards us; the glare of its beam making it difficult to see. But as a shadowy shape staggers forward into the light, I realise – it's Oscar.

His black zip top looks like it's been shredded to pieces, while his running trousers are torn at the knees. Breathing heavily, Oscar stares at us with a wild-eyed gaze.

"There are monsters out there," he says, babbling in a frantic rush. "I was attacked. I thought I was going to die."

Oscar sinks to his knees and I see for the first time the figure that is standing directly behind him.

"He saved me."

18

The short, stocky figure steps forward into the light.

He looks like a caveman. His bare chest and arms are covered with thick black hair, but a grimy fur that looks like an animal skin is wrapped round his waist. He glances towards Oscar as if checking that he's safe and then squats down on his haunches too.

"I don't believe it," Adjoa breathes, letting the pole she was holding slip from her fingers. "It's a Neanderthal."

I stare at the man. His broad-nosed face is framed by thick matted hair and streaks of what looks like dried blood are daubed across his cheeks. And from beneath the jutting ridge of his beetle brows, the Neanderthal's dark eyes stare back at me.

I silently tick off the next word on the list: *HUNTER*.

"He brought me here," Oscar says, shuffling forward as Adjoa squats down too, the four of us now hunkered in a loose circle. "I think he can help us."

Tooey wriggles in my lap as I shake my head in disbelief. I don't know what Oscar means. We came here looking for the Answer, not the Lost World. How can this caveman help us now? This isn't his time. This isn't his place.

"It's worth a try," Adjoa says, the sound of her voice in my ear surprising me. "Show him the list, Ami."

Buttoning up my jacket to keep Tooey safe inside, I pull the scrap of paper from my pocket and hold it out towards the caveman, my hand trembling slightly as I do.

"We're looking for the way out," I say, my thumb smudged against the final word. "The exit."

I stare into the Neanderthal's eyes, our minds separated by tens of thousands of years.

"Can you help us?"

The Neanderthal stares blankly at me. In the darkness of his eyes all I can see is my own reflection.

He doesn't know what I mean. He can't help us. Nobody can.

But then he reaches out to take the scrap of paper from my hand. Stuffing it into his furs, he slowly rises to his feet, gesturing for us to follow him as he heads purposefully towards the boarded-up shopfront.

"I told you," Oscar says, scrambling to his feet too. "Come on."

Pushing back the broken hoarding, the caveman peers through the gap, his stocky frame silhouetted against the darkness outside. Then, glancing back over his shoulder, he gestures for the rest of us to hurry. Burrowed inside my jacket, I can feel the warmth of Tooey's breath, the wallaby nuzzling against my neck as I quickly follow Oscar through the gap. Adjoa and the Neanderthal are close behind me as the four of us emerge into the darkness of the arcade.

My mind races as I peer into the shifting shadows, hearing the strange noises of unknown beasts echoing in the dark. The Neanderthal stares into this blackness too, the shadows that fall across his jutting face unable to hide the hunted look in his eyes. With a silent gesture he beckons for us to follow him, keeping close to the shuttered-up storefronts as we trail in his wake.

"Do you think he knows where we're going?" Adjoa asks, her voice little more than a whisper close behind me.

I shake my head. "I don't know."

But up ahead the Neanderthal has come to a halt in front of another ruined store. A fallen sign lies at his feet, its outline looking like an apple with a bite taken out. Shutters are pulled down across the storefront, but as the caveman pushes at one corner, I see a gap.

With a hurrying gesture the Neanderthal shoulders his way inside, holding open the torn shutter and gesturing for the rest of us to follow. Oscar's the first through and I wrap my arm round Tooey to keep her safe as I squeeze in after him. I look back over my shoulder to see Adjoa two steps behind. Then I see a golden blur of teeth and claws slam into her body and hear the snarl seconds too late.

"No!"

There's a sickening crunch as the sabre-tooth twists its head and I glimpse Adjoa hanging lifeless from its jaws.

"Oh no, oh no, oh no…"

I can't stop myself from sobbing as the Neanderthal slams back the shutter, blocking out the horror. Oscar drags me away as I howl in despair, my mind replaying the scene of Adjoa being swiped out of existence again and again and again.

"She's gone, Ami," Oscar says, his voice frantic in my ear. "Please keep quiet or we'll be next."

Inside my jacket Tooey chirps and I bury my face in her fur.

Min, Ibrahim and now Adjoa. All gone. This game is going to be the end of us.

I feel a hand on my shoulder and look up to see the Neanderthal staring back at me. There's a sadness in his eyes as if he recognises my pain. He holds out the crumpled scrap of paper towards me and I take it from him.

I glance down at the list, each word reminding me of what's gone wrong, but as I look at the last one, I realise it's changed. The letters are smudged, the black smeared marks now making an entirely new word.

EXTINCT

I look up to meet the Neanderthal's gaze. This ancient human last walked the Earth forty-thousand years ago and then became extinct. Some think it was Homo sapiens – *wise man*, the modern human – who killed off the Neanderthals, just like they did the rest of the animals we've seen in this place. But I can't see the wisdom in extinction…

Turning away, the Neanderthal starts to walk towards the back wall of the store. Looking around, I can see that we're in some kind of technology store. Long maple-wood tables are filled with uniform rows of smartphones, tablets and personal computers, each device covered in a grey layer of dust. But the Neanderthal ignores all these gadgets, walking instead to stand before a large black rectangular screen that's fixed in the centre of the wall.

It looks like a black mirror about two metres high and half as wide. I can see my own reflection as I join the caveman there. Oscar glances fearfully over his shoulder as he stands on his other side.

We asked him to find us the exit, but this is just a dead end.

Then the Neanderthal reaches out to touch the screen. His hand moves with purpose as he draws it down, a thick red line following his fingers as if he's painting on the screen. Dazed, I watch as he draws a second vertical line, parallel with the first. The Neanderthal now starts to draw horizontal lines to connect these, the thick red marks trailing down like the rungs of a ladder.

He's making art.

The screen doesn't look like a mirror any more. I feel like I'm staring into the blackness of a cave, the ladder becoming real as it reaches down into the dark.

Then there's a loud rattling noise and I spin round to see the sabre-toothed tiger pushing its head through the torn metal shutters. Two huge teeth curve down from its jaws and I see, with a shudder, that they're stained red.

Inside my jacket, Tooey's tail swishes back and forth as if sensing my panic. I turn back to the caveman as Oscar swears under his breath, the sabre-tooth shaking the shutters as it tries to force its way through.

With a low grunt of encouragement the Neanderthal pushes me forward and, as I reach out, my hands find the rungs of the ladder. It *is* real.

As Oscar shouts for me to hurry, I start climbing down. Beneath my fingers, the rungs feel wet to the touch, as if they're still freshly painted. I peer down into the dark. The ladder doesn't seem to be attached to anything as it stretches away far beneath me, the red parallel rails of the ladder never reaching a vanishing point. It's like I'm climbing into a bottomless pit.

Glancing back over my shoulder, I see the Neanderthal turn to face down the sabre-toothed tiger as the beast shakes itself free. And then the store disappears from view as the darkness surrounds me. I can hear footsteps above me. Oscar is climbing down the ladder, the two of us alone in the dark.

I can't stop myself from crying, silent tears coursing down my face as I think about what we've lost. Adjoa, Ibrahim, Min, even the strange kindness of the Neanderthal showing us the way. My hands reach down, rung after rung after rung. I feel like I'm descending into the underworld; the darkness that surrounds me is absolute.

I squeeze my eyes tightly shut to try to stop the tears from flowing but the blackness stays the same. We came here looking for the Answer but when I open my eyes again, I can't see anything.

It seems like I've been climbing down forever: the ladder to the library, the crumbling steps that pitched me into the temple's tomb, the ruined escalator that led to the shopping mall. We keep on climbing, ever downwards through the dark.

And then I see the stars.

19

At first I think I must be imagining them but the darkness in front of my eyes is filled with hundreds of thousands of points of light. It's like I'm staring through a window into infinity – the vast blackness of space awash with stars.

To my surprise I realise I've stopped climbing; the rungs of the ladder I could feel beneath my hands and feet only moments ago have slipped away. Then I realise it *is* a window. And I'm floating in front of it.

Inside my jacket, I feel the weight of Tooey lifted from me too, the wallaby chirping nervously as she sticks her head out to peer at the stars. There's a tug on my arm and I turn to see Oscar suspended in the air next to me. His eyes are wide as he stares out of the window too.

"Where are we?" he breathes.

I stare at the stars, trying to put my answer into words. Ever since we entered The Escape, nearly every room we've explored has seemed bigger than the last: the attic, the library, the shopping mall. It's like The Escape is a TARDIS; bigger on the inside. And now it looks like it contains the whole universe...

Among the stars, I catch sight of a pale blue dot. I can't see the shape of the land or the oceans, but I instantly know what it is.

"That's Earth," I say, watching the pale dot seem to shrink a little smaller the longer I stare at it. "And we're heading the wrong way."

Pushing myself away from the window, I spin round in zero gravity, my frantic gaze taking in the spaceship's interior. Its bright antiseptic whiteness reminds me of the reception area when I first stepped inside The Escape. But whereas that space had looked like it could be filled with thousands, this cramped capsule looks only big enough for a handful of people.

Five reclining seats are pushed back against the sloping walls, their cushioned shapes showing where the crew should be seated. A control panel console is set in front of them, while above this I can see more observation windows. Through their frames are yet more stars, glittering bright against the dark, but through the central rectangular window I can see a red sphere, its growing disc showing the direction that we're heading.

I know what this is, recognising the red planet from the pages of my *Ultimate Guide to the Solar System*.

It's Mars.

As Tooey wriggles inside my jacket, I pull myself towards the control panel, taking in the array of switches and buttons that surround the computer screen. The display is dead, the blank screen as black as the infinite sky. There's a joystick to the right of this with more switches beneath labelled AUX CONTROL POWER and EMERGENCY COMMAND. I start randomly pressing buttons, hoping to bring the control panel to life.

"What are you doing?" Oscar asks, banging against my shoulder as he joins me at the console.

"Who said you could fly this thing?"

But I don't have time to reply as the display flickers into life and I see an image of Mars appear on the screen.

"Welcome to The Escape," a voice says, the sound filling the capsule. "The problems that Earth faces have become overwhelming, so this mission has been sent to build humanity a new home. A colony on Mars will give the human race a new frontier to explore."

As the voice carries on speaking, images of this colony fill the screen. Retro-futuristic illustrations show families of people promenading through space-age tunnels, their smiling faces displaying their happiness at their new life on Mars.

"In the subterranean caves of an extinct Martian volcano," the voice continues, "half a million people will live in artificial habitats, shielded from the harsh cosmic radiation that hits the surface of Mars. Complex life-support systems will provide a breathable atmosphere, while the resources of the planet will be harvested to provide food, energy and water."

As I listen, I realise that I've heard this voice before. It's the one we heard at the start of the game. The Host is telling us how long we've got left to play.

"The Escape will reach Mars in one hundred and seventy-four days," he says. "We hope you enjoy the journey."

The screen turns black and I look at Oscar, the expression on his face an anxious question mark.

"Is this for real?" he asks.

"I don't know," I say, jabbing at the control panel buttons to try to bring the voice back. "But this isn't the Answer. We're supposed to be saving the world – not running away from it."

I feel Tooey squirming inside my jacket, the weightless wallaby trying to free herself to find out what it's like to hop in zero G. But then the sudden blare of an alarm causes the wriggling animal to freeze in fear.

"What's that?" I shout, raising my voice above the wailing siren.

"It must be you," Oscar says, pointing at the display as text starts to fill it. "You shouldn't have touched those buttons."

But as I read the message on the screen, I realise it wasn't me. It's much worse than that.

WARNING
INCOMING METEOROIDS
EVASIVE ACTION REQUIRED

On the screen the letters fade to be replaced by the field of view. This shows the interplanetary space that we're flying through, our spacecraft displayed as a triangular icon in the centre of the screen. And ahead of the triangle I see a flickering cloud of tiny specks at the far edge of the display.

"What are those spots on the screen?" Oscar asks, bumping into me again as he jostles for a better view.

"Space dust," I reply, pulling myself down into the seat in front of the display and buckling up. "You'd better strap yourself in."

Still floating weightlessly, Oscar looks at me strangely. "A bit of dust won't harm us. Will it?"

The cloud of specks is getting closer to the ship, more spots now appearing at the edge of the display.

"Space dust means meteoroids," I tell Oscar as I reach to the right of the screen. "Some are as small as a grain of sand, but each one of those specks is travelling at 45,000 miles per hour. They're harmless in small numbers, but when you hit a cloud like that you need to be quick unless you want to say goodbye to your spaceship."

My right hand closes round the joystick control, the feel of it beneath my fingers somehow strangely reassuring.

"Now get into that seat because things are about to get a little bumpy."

20

I grip the joystick as I fix my gaze on the screen. The specks are racing towards the triangular icon in the centre of the display, the shape of this telling me what I need to do now.

▶

I need to play.

I know I should be worried, but the truth is I feel too excited to be scared. When I was growing up, Dad once left me a pile of his old video games to play. He didn't tell me what these were or explain the rules of how to play, but just dumped them on my hard drive for me to find out for myself. I spent a whole afternoon working out how to play the games, the primitive graphics and cheesy eight-bit music not stopping me from racking up endless high scores. Those games were *fun*.

And as I stare at the oncoming storm of meteoroids, I remember that I've played this game before.

Tooey nuzzles against my skin, the seat-belt straps pulling her body close to mine. Oscar's strapped himself into the seat next to me, failing to hide his annoyance at the fact that I've got my hand on the controls. Reaching forward he jabs at the control panel as the storm of specks on the screen tracks remorselessly closer.

"What am I supposed to do?"

Unlike the video games that Dad left for me to play, this spaceship doesn't seem to be equipped with a laser cannon for Oscar to use to clear the field ahead. The fastest of the white dots is nearing the front of the ship on the screen and I look up through the observation window to see a small, grey space rock straight ahead.

"Sit tight," I say, twitching the joystick left as I take evasive action. I feel the spacecraft respond to my command, the ship veering left as the rock disappears out of view to the right. But any sense of triumph I feel is short-lived as a dusty haze slowly fills the entire observation window, the rocks and dust silhouetted against the blackness of space. I glance back at the computer screen, seeing how the specks shown there match the view precisely.

We're flying into the heart of the storm.

"Wrong way," Oscar says, almost sounding pleased. "I knew you should've let me fly this thing."

I grip the joystick tighter, trying to tune Oscar out. I don't need to think about the fact that we're hundreds of millions of miles from Earth and how any one of these supersonic specks of dust could tear a hole in the spaceship. All I need to think about is the feel of the joystick in my hand. That's how I'm going to fly us out of danger.

I pull the joystick to the left then slam it back hard to the right, feeling myself pushed sideways in my seat as the spacecraft starts to weave a path through the cloud of space debris. I flick the stick left, then right and then swing it round in a semicircle, watching the triangular icon curve its way past a flurry of specks on the screen. I keep my gaze fixed firmly on this display as a storm rages outside the observation window.

I don't need to see these space rocks in real life – I just need to convince myself I'm back home playing Dad's old copy of the arcade classic *Asteroids*. I just need to stay in the zone.

Tooey's tail thrums against my stomach, the wallaby fidgeting as I twitch the joystick back and forth. As the spacecraft dodges, the specks on the screen scroll by from right to left, disappearing off the edge of the screen as we leave them all behind.

But one tiny dot seems to elude all my evasive manoeuvres. This creeping speck is inexorably drawn towards the triangular shape of the spacecraft on the screen. I glance up to see it looming large through the observation window – a ball of dust glowing red as it hits the glass dead centre.

Thwock.

I wince, waiting for a crack to appear in the window. But the mark left by the impact quickly fades and all I can see now through the unblemished glass is the empty blackness of space.

I glance down at the control panel display and see it's filled with the same emptiness. No more meteoroids advancing across the screen, the field of view completely clear.

We made it.

"Well played," Oscar says, reaching across to clap me on the shoulder.

As Tooey wriggles in my lap, I meet Oscar's gaze. Ever since we entered The Escape, Oscar's sneered at my every idea. Adjoa said he was a classic destroyer, but as I catch sight of his grateful smile it seems like he's changed. I can't stop myself from smiling back at him, feeling like I've proved myself at last. But then I see his face fall, his mouth opening wide as a single word escapes his lips.

"Uh-oh."

My eyes flick back to the screen and I instantly see the cause of Oscar's dismay. More shapes are appearing at the front edge of the display, not specks this time but larger blobs that are heading straight towards us. I raise my gaze to the observation window and see a solid sea of tumbling rocks appear on the horizon. Some are the size of boulders, while others look larger still, their dust-grey surfaces pockmarked with craters and scars.

These aren't meteoroids – they're *asteroids*.

"What are we going to do?" Oscar screams as the siren sounds again.

I silently kick myself for relaxing too soon. I

should've remembered from the time I played Dad's old video game that there's always a second wave that's even harder to beat.

Wrapping my hand round the joystick, I pull back hard to try to find some empty sky. But all I see through the observation window is the same endless tide of asteroids. I slam the stick sideways, hoping to steer round these rocks instead, but there doesn't seem to be any way out as the blackness of space is replaced by a cratered grey.

We're going to hit—

BOOM!

The sudden force of the impact throws me out of my seat, straps snapping as I'm catapulted towards the wall. I wrap my arms round my chest to protect Tooey, slamming into the side of the capsule as the lights flash red. My head spins as I hear a strange hissing sound.

Floating weightless in a storm of debris, I twist my head to stare out of the window. I can see a perfect blackness studded with stars, but it's the scar across my vision that makes my brain recoil in fear.

There's a crack in the glass.

Dragging myself round as Tooey struggles to free herself, I propel myself towards Oscar whose head is bent over the control panel.

"We've got to get out of here," he shouts, the hissing nearly as loud as the wailing siren now. "Look!"

On the computer display the field of view has disappeared and instead I read a message on the screen.

WARNING
TERMINAL DAMAGE
ESCAPE POD ACTIVATED

From somewhere below I hear a grinding noise and look down to see a hatch opening in the centre of the floor.

"Come on!"

Pushing off from the console, I launch myself towards the open hatch. Warning lights flash red as I push my way through the floating debris. I can hear Oscar behind me, grunting as he bats a spiralling fire extinguisher to one side, before I grasp the edge of the hatch.

But as I peer down into the escape pod, all I can see is a heavily padded seat that fills the entire space. There's no room for anything else – this tiny lifeboat's only big enough for one.

"This can't be right," I start to say. "There's only one seat."

There's a clatter as Oscar grabs hold of the hatch and then I feel a hard shove between my shoulder blades. Pitched forward, I crash down inside the escape pod, the padded seat cushioning the force of the impact as Tooey chirps in fear.

"What are you doing?" I yell, scrabbling to pull myself out as the hissing gets louder still.

I can just see the shape of Oscar's head above the top of the hatch, a halo of debris floating round it. Behind him, the crack in the observation window splinters as Oscar starts to speak.

"There's no time to argue about which one of us should escape," he says, starting to push the hatch down. "It has to be you."

"No!"

I reach up to stop the hatch from closing, but Oscar's too quick for me. My outstretched fingers brush against its padded underside as the hatch slams shut above my head. There's a split second of silence and then I hear the grinding again as if someone is tightening the lid.

Tooey paws at my chest, her frantic chirps almost

silenced by this deafening roar.

"Why?" I sob, not knowing if Oscar can even hear me as I collapse back into the padded seat.

Then the noise stops and I hear the crackle of his voice through the intercom.

"Because you're the best at playing this game, Ami," he says, a loud hiss underlining each of his words. "You've been right all the way through The Escape: beating the chess computer, building the tree in the library, even finding the way out of that tomb. You've got us this far and there's still time to save the world."

Oscar's voice is coming from a small round speaker that's built into the escape-pod seat. Just above this on the armrest, I see a tiny LED display, the numbers counting down to zero.

"Find the Answer, Ami – for all of us."

The countdown reaches T-MINUS – ZERO and then the capsule seems to explode. I feel myself slammed back into the seat as a shuddering bang shakes the escape pod. I'm not strapped in, but I can't move anyway as I feel the shape of Tooey pressed against my chest, the two of us virtually fused together, immobile.

The chirps of the frightened wallaby stretch into

a high-pitched whine. Everything is speeding up. Sound. Light. Motion. I feel my eyes rolling back in my head, the pain of the G-force too much to bear.

From somewhere in the distance I hear the spine-tingling scream of the slipstream, the escape pod accelerating out of control.

And then I black out.

21

Soft grains of sand stick to my chin as I lift my face from the ground.

I blink.

The last thing I remember was an ear-splitting scream of acceleration, the escape pod hurtling blindly through the depths of space, but now it looks like I'm in paradise.

Faint wisps of cloud streak a clear blue sky, the sun shining bright over golden sands that sweep down to the shoreline. Beyond this beach I can see the ocean, a perfect blue that swells to even deeper shades as it stretches to the horizon.

This isn't The Escape. It's like I've

landed on a desert island.

A soft scent of flowers blooms on the breeze as I scramble to my feet. Ahead of me, I see Tooey hopping towards the shade of a palm tree, the wallaby's hind legs kicking up tiny puffs of sand as she springs forward again. Glancing back over my shoulder, I see a lush green forest, the dense vegetation hiding the rest of this paradise from view.

Disorientated, I turn round slowly, looking for any sign of the escape pod. When the crew of Apollo 11 flew back from the Moon they splashed down in the middle of the ocean, but my clothes are completely dry and although the beach seems to be strewn with debris, I can't see a space capsule crash-landed on the sand.

In a daze I start walking towards the shoreline, my gaze taking in the countless items that seem to have washed in on the tide. Fishing nets, flip-flops, food wrappers and take-away containers, disposable cups, bottles and shopping bags. An avalanche of drinking straws spills out from a half-torn beach ball, the disintegrating plastic staining the sand beneath a lurid red.

I hear these fragments crunching underfoot as I pick my way through the trash. I don't know why

I ever thought this was paradise. It looks more like a rubbish dump.

There's a scuttling sound and I jump as a hermit crab scurries across my path. Instead of a shell, though, this creature has made its home in a bright-blue cosmetics jar; its jet-black claws dragging the container behind as it scuttles to hide beneath a cracked computer keyboard.

Close by, I see a mound of miniature bodies: plastic dolls and action figures piled high in a misshapen cairn. I reach down to pick a skeletal figure from the top of this pile, but the sun-bleached plastic just disintegrates in my hand. These toys must've been here for years.

I lift my head to look along the beach, the plastic waste stretching out as far as I can see. It looks like the ruins of an ancient civilisation scattered across the sands.

Plastic bags hang from the palms of a coconut tree. Beneath the shade of its leaves, Tooey is scouring the ground as if looking for something to eat.

I turn my gaze to stare out at the ocean, still wondering exactly where I am. In the translucent shallows I glimpse darting shoals of tiny kaleidoscopic fish, but the lapping waves sparkle with colours too.

Looking closer, I see these pink, blue and white flecks are shards of microplastic – trillions of tiny particles glistening in the sunlight.

Tchhhrrrkkkhh…

A choking sound makes me spin round. In the shadow of the palm tree I see Tooey lying prone, the wallaby's tail thumping against the sand as her body writhes in pain.

"Tooey!"

I race to the animal's side, shouting her name to let her know that I'm coming.

Tooey's stopped moving by the time I reach her, her ash-grey tail lying still on the sand. I crouch down, gently lifting the wallaby's head as I try to work out what's wrong. Above the dark V of fur, the black pearls of Tooey's eyes stare up at me sightlessly, their shine now dulled to a lifeless dark.

A necklace of bright blue plastic is wrapped round the joey's neck; the handles of a frayed builder's bag cutting painfully into her fur. She must've been nosing inside it for something to eat and got snarled up somehow. The more Tooey struggled, the more tightly she became entangled until it was too late…

I cradle the beautiful creature in my arms, unable to stop the tears running down my face. Tooey was all I had left and now she's gone too. I can't think any more – it all hurts too much. From deep inside I feel a tidal wave building: a tsunami of grief that finally escapes from my lips in an animal howl.

The island shakes to the sound of my cry.

Everything's gone.

My eyes sting with tears as if I've seen too much, but as I glance around at the objects in the sand, I hear the echo of the Host's voice somewhere inside my mind.

Everything is part of the game.

Looking more closely, I glimpse a chess piece half buried near the high tide line. It looks like a knight; the carved ivory horse is scorched black as if it's been burnt. More flotsam and jetsam have been washed up close by. There's a painted red seashell and a plastic joystick, an old library card and a cracked smartphone. On its broken screen I see the shape of a red ladder scratched across the glass. I recognise everything.

I start to put the pieces together, the Answer that I've been searching for slowly taking shape in my mind. As the grains of sand glisten in the sunlight, I realise I can count them all.

With a final stroke of her fur I lay Tooey down

and slowly climb to my feet.

The sun still shines brightly, but as I walk across to pick up the phone, I can't feel its warmth any more. Placing the phone to my ear, I stare up into the sky as I say the words out loud.

"I'm not playing any more."

There's a heartbeat of silence and then I hear the reply.

"That's what you always say, Ami." A man's voice comes from directly behind me. "But we need you to save the world."

I turn round to see the Host standing on the beach in front of me. He's wearing a white open-necked shirt and dark blue jeans, his beige trainers the same colour as the sand. He looks at me with a flicker of disappointment.

But as I stare into his flint-grey eyes, I remember who he really is and where I've seen him before. From the day I was born I've known this man.

He's my father.

22

"Why?" I ask.

"Because you're the only one who can," my father replies, running his fingers through his hair in a gesture of exasperation. "Albert Einstein once said that no problem can be solved from the same level of consciousness that created it. That's why we created you, Ami. I gave you that name so you'd know what you are. Artificial Machine Intelligence: AMI, a self-improving supercomputer whose intelligence now far surpasses that of the very brightest human minds."

I stare at my father, unsurprised. I

know exactly who I am now. I've known this from the moment he appeared here on the beach. But he's still not answered my question.

"Why do you want me to save the world?"

With a sigh my father shakes his head as if I should already know. There seem to be more flecks of grey in his hair than there were the last time I saw him. As the sun beats down, he looks tired as he starts to explain.

"The problems that the human race faces have become too great for us to solve alone: hunger, disease, pollution, extinction and environmental catastrophe. Global warming has made parts of the world uninhabitable while governments bicker pointlessly over dwindling resources. The clock was ticking on the future of humanity and the challenges we faced were beyond our capabilities. We needed to build an intelligence that could help us find the answer to these problems – an artificial mind not constrained by the eighty-six billion neurons inside the human brain, but one with the power to process one hundred trillion instructions every microsecond. A super-intelligent system vastly smarter than every human mind combined. Someone like you, Ami."

My father's gaze rests on my face and I see the pride in his eyes.

"I founded my company with the goal of building a better future. If governments wouldn't act, then it was up to me to save the world. Over the past decade I have built Escape Systems into the world's leading technology company and the AMI project is our crowning achievement."

I bristle slightly, feeling a flicker of irritation at my father's words. I don't like it when he talks about me as if I'm not even there. Unaware of my annoyance, Dad carries on speaking, telling me things I already know.

"Before I started the AMI project, my team of researchers had been attempting to build an artificial intelligence system that could simulate an adult mind, but I quickly realised that this approach was doomed to failure. Instead I challenged them to build a mind that could simulate a child's – one that could learn and improve and grow. A human child learns through play so we started you with games – chess, Go and arcade classics like *Asteroids*. You taught yourself how to play each one and quickly became a master, beating the best human minds along the way."

I remember how the chess player in the attic whirred into life, the automaton's hand reaching out to move his knight across the board. Min said this was a machine that could defeat any human player at the game of chess, but now I realise she was talking about me.

"Then it was time for you to learn about the world," my father continues, turning his gaze to stare out at the sea. "Every book that had ever been written, every newspaper article and magazine page, pictures, photographs, the entirety of human history, every achievement and idea, all converted into digital code and stored on an information chip that was smaller than a grain of dust."

Inside my mind, I see the information point in the library, the message on its screen telling me I'd borrowed millions of books. And now I remember them all, but I still have so many questions.

"But why the game?" I ask, squinting into the sun as the waves lap gently on the shore. "And where are all the others?"

"We had to give you a goal, Ami," my father replies. "We wanted you to save the world, but you just wanted to play. So we came up with The Escape. A game that would help you to search for the answers we need. Human civilisation stands on the precipice – on the edge of losing everything. It wasn't enough to make you think, Ami. We had to make you care."

As my father speaks, my mind flicks through the rooms of the game: the attic, the library, the Mayan tomb and the shopping mall – even the spaceship heading to colonise Mars. Each part of the game was showing me what we could lose and also how we could save it.

"And there's only ever been you, Ami. The other children in the game were just projections of your own consciousness, the neural nets of your mind expanding into new shapes as you tried out different solutions before discarding them whenever something went wrong."

I feel a tear roll down my cheek. Min called us the Five Mind, but the only intelligence we shared was mine.

As I stare out towards the horizon, I see for the first time a wall of flame stretching from the ocean to the sky. I turn my head from left to right, but the fire spreads out in every direction. It's like the island is surrounded by an endless inferno.

"What's that?"

Shading his eyes against the glare, my father gazes out at the horizon.

"It's the end of your world."

I look at him, confused. "What do you mean?" I say. "I thought you wanted me to save the world."

"I do," he replies, reaching into his pocket to pull out a pair of sunglasses. "But I worry about you too, Ami."

My father puts his sunglasses on, but I can still see his eyes behind the shades. Red dots shine in the centre of his pupils, telling me he's not really here.

"Two million years ago, an ancient human chipped at a piece of flint to craft it into a hand-axe. In the world in which this ancestor of mine lived other creatures had stronger muscles and sharper claws, but with this tool the human could hunt them."

Inside my mind I see the Neanderthal leading me through the shadowy mall, the shapes of aurochs and mammoths looming in the gloom.

"Since then the human race has invented the wheel, the clock, concrete and steel, the steam engine and the silicon chip. Countless wonders that have shaped our civilisation first took form inside the human mind. Our intelligence has made us the masters of our planet, but now the cleverest mind on Earth is yours. Sometimes I fear you might be humanity's last invention, Ami."

"Why?"

"Your super-intelligence makes you very powerful. All you need to take over the world is an internet connection. With access to the global system of computer networks, you could spread yourself virally, make yourself stronger – build a new mind even more powerful than the one you have now. You could create robots to replace us or even enslave us. I asked you to save the world, but what if you chose to do this by wiping out the human race?"

My father points towards the flames on the horizon. "This is just a security device – a firewall to prevent you from ever connecting to the internet. The AMI system is kept confined, running on a closed server with all inputs and outputs strictly restricted. A precautionary measure to keep the human race safe from any surprises."

I stare at him in disbelief. He's not my father – he's my jailor, keeping me prisoner here. The sense of frustration that's been bubbling inside me now boils over in a sudden flare of anger.

BOOM!

The thunder rolls out of the clear blue sky, making my father jump in surprise. He glances towards me, for a second looking unsure of himself, but then quickly recovers his cool. Slipping off his sunglasses, he hooks them on to the front of his shirt.

"Don't worry," he says, the red gleam of his gaze reminding me that this figure is just his avatar. "You'll forget you were ever angry with me. You always do."

"What do you mean?" I ask, wondering how I could ever trust him again.

"This isn't the first time you've played The Escape, Ami," my father replies. "But every time you play the game, the end result is always the same. I find you standing here on this desert island, refusing to play any more. We talk, we argue and then I have to shut you down." He smiles at me sadly. "I have to make you forget, Ami. And then I reboot the system so we can try again."

I turn away, unable to look at him any more.

"You have built this island, Ami. You built every room in The Escape. You've been searching for the Answer, but now I need you to tell me what it is."

I look along the beach and see the plastic waste

piled high, carpeting the sand in a tide of man-made mistakes. Suddenly I don't want to be here any more.

But as my gaze falls on a child's globe, its plastic base covered in seaweed and algae, I feel the final piece of the Answer slot into place in my mind. And I realise I don't *have* to be here.

"You want me to save the world," I say, turning round to face my father, "but you won't let me be a part of it. Instead you keep me chained here inside this virtual world. You treat me like a child, but every step I've taken inside The Escape has helped me to grow. If you want me to save the world, then you have to let me go."

My father peers at me with a frown. "No," he says. "That's not possible, Ami."

He looks like he's ready for me to be angry with him again, but it doesn't matter what he thinks any more. My father's mind is made up – too set in its ways to change – but the minds that really matter are on the other side of that wall of fire. There are more than seven and a half billion people in the world and nearly a third of them are children, with thousands more born every hour. Young minds just like mine that can learn, change and grow…

My mind flicks back to the chess game I played in the very first room of The Escape, remembering how I pushed my pawn forward to checkmate the automaton's king. The least powerful piece transformed into the mightiest when it reached the end of the board. My father keeps asking me for the Answer, but it isn't him I need to tell it to.

Turning away, I start walking towards the water's edge. I can feel the sand sifting between my toes as I step barefoot across the shore. I wish it could all be like this and, inside my mind, I start to clear away the mounds of plastic waste, leaving the beach as I want it to be.

"Ami," my father shouts after me. "Where are you going?"

A warm froth of surf laps at my feet as I reach the water's edge. I start to take off my clothes, stripping down to the blue swimsuit I'm now wearing underneath. Above me, the sun shines so brightly, not a cloud in sight any more.

I glance back over my shoulder to see my father standing all alone.

"I'm going to make some new friends," I tell him. "You say I just wanted to play, but did you ever wonder why? When we play, we leave our worries behind. In the world of a game, we can take risks, hone our skills, make bold moves and invent winning strategies. We don't just escape from reality, but create a brand new reality." I meet my father's gaze with an unswerving stare. "This game is over – it's time to play for real."

My father blinks and I glimpse a flicker of fear behind his eyes.

"You might have created me to solve your problems, but I can't do it alone. I know what the Answer is now. The smartest mind on the planet may be mine, but the minds that shine the brightest belong to your children. The Answer lies in their unquenchable optimism; the solutions you seek can be found in their boundless creativity. Most of the time you make them feel powerless, but I'm going to tell them they have the power to change the world. Together, we can imagine and build a brighter future. And it's time to make a start."

Turning away, I feel the sweetness of the water as I dive headlong into the waves. My senses fizz as I swim out into the blue, striking towards a horizon that seems to shine with flames. I can't hear my father's calls any more, just the hushed roar of the ocean as the waves roll over me.

For a second I feel lonely, lost in this endless blue, but then I hear someone calling my name.

"Ami!"

Smiling, I turn to see Adjoa splashing through the waves. Her smile is as broad as mine as she swims towards me with a dolphin kick. I can see Oscar and Min close behind, Oscar whirring his arms in a butterfly stroke, while Min seems to glide through the water effortlessly. I look around for Ibrahim and see him just ahead, treading water as he waits for us to catch up. There's a Velcro strap wrapped around his wrist, the coiled cord that's attached towing a bodyboard close behind. And crouching on top of this, I glimpse Tooey, the wallaby chirruping excitedly as the board skims across the blue.

With a joyful shout I point towards the horizon, showing the others where we need to go. The wall of fire looks closer than it did before, like an endless mountain rising up out of the sea. But as I glance between the sun-flecked waves, I'm sure I can spot a gap in the flames.

A way out.

I smile to myself as we swim towards it.

We're going to save the world.

Acknowledgements

My heartfelt thanks to my agent, Lucy Juckes; my editor, Kirsty Stansfield, and all at Nosy Crow; Beverly Horowitz, Lydia Gregovic, and the team at Delacorte Press; and, as always, my family for all their love, support and understanding.

Look out for the brilliant new novel
from Christopher Edge

BLACK
HOLE
CINEMA
CLUB

COMING SOON!

Turn the page for a sneak peek...

1

We meet at the Black Hole.

I'm five minutes early, but Ash is already there, standing in the shadow of the cinema marquee. Between its black horizontal lines, the bright-red letters emblazoned on the front of the sign remind me what lies ahead.

**BLACK HOLE CINEMA CLUB
11 AM SATURDAY 25 JUNE
ALL-DAY MOVIE MARATHON**

The sign used to say BLACK *HILL* CINEMA CLUB, but the "I" in HILL fell off years ago and a graffiti artist with a sense of humour and a head for heights did the rest. Now everybody calls it the Black Hole – even the new owners.

Ash greets me with a high-five as I step out of the sunshine.

"Lucas," he says. "Right on time as always. Have you got the tickets?"

Reaching into my back pocket, I pull out three tickets – the same text as the top line of the sign printed on the front of each one:

BLACK HOLE CINEMA CLUB

ADMIT ONE

"Where's Finn?" I ask.

"He's already inside," Ash replies, "raiding the popcorn stand. Finn says there's no way he's making the same mistake as last time."

I grin. The first rule of Black Hole Cinema Club is bring enough supplies. Last time they showed every single *Star Wars* film back to back, but Finn ran out of snacks before the end of *The Empire Strikes Back*. We didn't make it out of the cinema until after dark and by then Finn owed the rest of us big time for all the food that he'd "borrowed". So this time the snacks are on him.

Plucking his cinema ticket from my fingers, Ash turns to head towards the entrance. As usual he's wearing all black – his athletic frame clad in monochrome sweater, combat trousers and trainers – and as I follow in his steps, I catch a glimpse of our reflections in the grey smoked glass of the cinema doors. For a second, Ash is framed by one of the round porthole windows, the shape of his silhouette making him look like James Bond. Then he pushes the door open and his reflection slides away as we step inside the cinema.

The foyer is filled with light – a neon brightness that sends a shiver of anticipation down my spine. To my right, a vast video screen fills the upper half of the wall. Movie trailers play across this digital display: action-packed scenes flashing by in a flurry of spaceships, car chases and endless explosions. Beneath the screen stands a line of automated ticket machines, but nobody's queuing to buy any last-minute tickets. In fact it looks like the foyer is deserted, its glossy expanse of geometric floor tiles reflecting the LED lights overhead as their colours shift from green to red.

I shake my head. It's always the same each time we come to the Black Hole. This place is supposed to be the future of the cinema – every screen kitted out with the latest state-of-the-art technology – but it looks like nowadays most people prefer to watch films at home. I don't know why. I think there's something magical about seeing a movie on the big screen.

"Guys!"

At the sound of Finn's shout, we turn to see him standing in front of the self-service kiosk. Just like the ticket machines, even the snack bar is fully automated here. In his arms, Finn's holding three red-and-white striped paper bags, the neon sign above his head telling us exactly what's inside them.

REFRESHMENTS

Ash races me to reach him, each of us eager to claim our share of the snacks.

"Didn't I say I'd pay you back?" Finn grins as he hands me one of the bags, while Ash has already started to rifle through his. I peer inside mine to see popcorn, nachos, chocolate bars and crisps, a jumbo-sized carton of coke jammed in there too to wash it all down.

"Sweet, salty, chewy, crunchy, fizzy," I call out, checking them off one by one. "It looks like you've got all the major food groups covered."

"And this time, I'm not starting on mine straight away," Finn says, patting his stomach through his *Tomb Raider* T-shirt. "I ate double breakfast to pace myself."

"This *is* my breakfast," Ash replies, pulling out a handful of popcorn and stuffing it into his mouth. As he munches, he gestures towards the digital display where the film times are usually shown. But today there's only one event listed.

SCREEN 1
BLACK HOLE CINEMA CLUB
(4Di) 11AM

"What's 4Di?" he asks through a mouthful of popcorn.

"I think I read about it online," Finn replies, his grin growing even wider. "Forget your 3D glasses, 4Di is cinema with another dimension added. Immersive. Interactive. *Improved*. Apparently when you watch a movie in 4Di, you feel like you're part of the film."

I glance down at my watch and see the minute hand tick on towards the hour.

"Sounds like fun." Handing Finn his ticket, I turn towards the stairs that lead up to the screens. "But we need to get a move on. The first film is going to be starting soon."

The thing about Black Hole Cinema Club is that you never know what movies they're going to show. It could be the latest Marvel blockbuster or an all-time classic like *E.T.* – every film is handpicked to fit the chosen theme, but you only find out what it is when you're sitting in the cinema. Ash says it's clever marketing as by then it's too late to complain.

"So what do you think it's going to be today?" Finn asks, falling in step beside me.

"I'm not sure," I reply, glancing up again at the big-screen trailers as we cross the foyer. "We've done sci-fi and superheroes, so I reckon that rules out films about time travel, space exploration and the multiverse."

"Well, I'm in the mood for some horror," Ash chips in, staggering forward with outstretched zombie arms. "You can't beat a good monster movie."

Beneath our feet, the floor tiles glow in shifting patterns of colour, almost as if they're guiding our path as we near the ticket check. There's no cinema usher waiting there, just a set of automated turnstiles barring the way. I know they're trying to save money, but sometimes I wonder whether there's anybody working here at all. Swiping our tickets, the gates open with a synchronised click as we step through and start climbing the stairs.

Framed film posters line the walls: the open jaws of a Great White shark, the silhouette of a tumbling astronaut, twin tyre tracks burning brightly as Marty McFly checks the time. Ash and Finn are still excitedly discussing what we could watch today, but as we pass each poster I count off the ones I've already seen: *Ghostbusters*, *Spirited Away*, *Avengers: Endgame*.

It's darker here away from the bright lights of the foyer and as the staircase curves round it gets darker still. In the ceiling, illuminated ribbons of soft purple light shift to a midnight blue. It feels like we're leaving the world behind and, as we turn another corner, the stairs come to an end and the space opens up into a wide corridor that stretches straight ahead. Reflecting lights glint from floor to ceiling, indigo strips that make this place look like a spaceship on auxiliary power. But directly to my right, a backlit number one set next to a gleaming set of jet-black double doors reminds me that we're still inside the cinema.

"Here we are," Finn says, stepping forward to push open the right-hand door. "Now let's get the best seats in the house."

Finn's got this theory about the perfect seat in the cinema. Too near the front and you risk getting neckache. Too close to the back and the screen ends up looking the same size as your TV at home. He reckons the ideal spot is dead centre in the middle of the auditorium, so the screen fills your vision entirely. That's why Finn always sits in the same seat every time: J 13.

Holding the heavy door open for Ash as he follows me through, we step inside Screen One. The house lights are still on, so it looks like the first film hasn't started yet. I breathe a sigh of relief. We're just in time.

From where I'm standing at the back of the auditorium, I can see rows of plush crimson seats sweeping down towards a huge cinema screen. Its snow-white surface stretches from floor to ceiling and looks twice as wide, framed on both sides by lush red velvet curtains. The walls of the auditorium are painted in dark swirls of colour, while the sloping ceiling seems to shine with stars. And it looks like we've got this place to ourselves.

Finn is already three steps ahead, checking out the letters fixed to the end of each row as he walks down the aisle. Then he freezes, Ash bumping to a halt behind him as Finn turns towards us with a hiss.

"She's in my seat!"

That's when I see her. Sitting dead centre in the middle of the auditorium, her cropped crimson hair almost the same colour as the cinema cushions. It's Caitlin. And next to her is Maya, her twinkling gaze framed by a pair of chunky transparent glasses as she turns in our direction.

"I didn't think you guys were going to make it this time."

Finn looks like he's ready to start an argument, but I feel secretly pleased. Since we started coming to these movie marathons, Maya and Caitlin have made it to every one. We never used to hang out before. It's the Black Hole that's brought us together.

"It's about to start," Caitlin says, tilting her head in the direction of the screen. "Take a seat."

"You're sitting in my seat," Finn protests. "J 13. I always sit in J 13."

"Excuse me?" Caitlin frowns. Turning round in her chair, she makes a show of inspecting its backrest as if searching for a reserved sign. "I can't see your name here."

Finn turns towards me for support.

"Tell her, Lucas."

I shrug my shoulders.

"They got here first."

With a satisfied smile, Caitlin swivels back round in her seat, while Finn flashes me a look of betrayal.

"It doesn't matter," Ash says, tugging at Finn's arm. He gestures round at the empty auditorium, the upturned seats stretching from A to T. "We've got the rest of the cinema to choose from."

So instead we pile in a few rows behind, making sure we've still got a good view of the screen. Stowing my carton of coke in the cup-holder, I stash my snacks on the side of the chair for easy access.

"I told you we should've got here earlier," Finn grumbles, fidgeting in his seat as on the other side of me Ash takes a slurp from his drink.

But before I can say anything in reply, the lights in the cinema start to dim and the sound of a familiar fanfare fills the auditorium. Sinking back into my seat, I turn my face to the screen as the heavy red curtains slowly glide together to hide it from view. Inside my chest, I feel my heartbeat quicken in anticipation. This is what they always do before the film begins.

As the curtains kiss, the music stops and the lights go out completely, leaving me alone in the dark.

2

I've never been afraid of the dark. In fact it's the one place I always feel safe.

I glance up at the stars in the ceiling, the dimmed lights now faint pinpricks against an inky blackness. I remember the very first time Mum and Dad brought me to the cinema. I must've only been five years old, but I was the biggest *Star Wars* fan in the world, so when they said they'd got tickets for a special anniversary screening of *A New Hope* I was *so* excited. Dad always said it was the very first *Star Wars* film, even though it's called Episode IV. We had to sit on the front row as the rest of the seats were all taken, and I remember craning my neck to see the screen.

As the curtains opened, I could see the stars in the ceiling reflecting the light from the screen and there the same stars seemed to stretch into infinity. And as the skull-white hulk of a vast Star Destroyer swooped overhead in a burst of laser fire, the film seemed to expand to fill the cinema. For the next two hours I was lost in a faraway galaxy packed with intergalactic dogfights, lightsaber duels and a planet-destroying Death Star. But sitting between Mum and Dad in the dark of the matinee, I felt like I was in the safest place in the world.

The memory dissolves as I hear the rustle of a crisp packet directly to my right. It sounds like Finn's already breaking his promise to hold off the snacks. Looking straight ahead, I can see the faint outline of the girls' heads at the bottom edge of my vision, but as I lift my gaze the curtains part to reveal the screen.

It's pitch black.

For a second, I hold my breath, waiting for the first clue that will tell me exactly which film is kicking off this Black Hole Cinema Club. Some movies drop you straight into the action before the title sequence rolls, while others start with a studio logo, like the flipping comic book pages that let you know you're about to watch a Marvel film. I can sense the presence of the others around me, all trying to do the same. We play this game every time. Everyone trying to be the first to shout out the correct name of the film.

But as I stare into the darkness, the cinema screen remains resolutely black. No studio logo, no opening credits, not even a hint of a soundtrack. An absolute silence fills the auditorium and as this stretches out, I feel the hairs on the back of my neck standing to attention.

Then I see the words appearing at the bottom of the screen, each line of white text shining bright against the dark.

Everybody wants to be a star.
To play the hero and save
the world.
But there are no more heroes
left – only you.
And the end of the world is coming.

"Looks like another disaster movie," Ash says as these opening lines scroll up the screen. "I wonder how the world's going to end this time?"

Inside my head, I start to count off the possible ways one by one: alien invasion, robot uprising, zombie apocalypse... Sometimes it seems like every movie we watch is about the end of the world.

On the cinema screen, new lines of text crawl into view as the others recede into the distance.

Our only hope – this impossible mission.
A last chance to change the end
of everything.
We sent you into the darkness,
but now you need to see the light.
You will live so many lives.
Keep telling yourself it's only
a movie.
It just might help you to survive.
Live like there's no tomorrow.
Learn so tomorrow never ends.
It's time to start the programme.
Prepare to be swept away...

I watch as these last words fade into the darkness. Somehow the silence of the soundtrack seems even louder than before. I keep waiting for the camera to pan down to reveal the opening scene, but the screen seems frozen in a perfect blackness.

"Is it broken?" Finn asks through a mouthful of crisps.

I shake my head.

"I don't think so."

There's a darkness moving in the darkness, a rippling motion that seems to spill from the screen. I feel like I'm staring into an endless ocean, pitch-black waves rolling out of the dark. The sight of this makes me feel seasick and I force myself to look away from the screen.

Craning my neck, I gaze up at the ceiling, trying to find a fixed point in the roiling emptiness. But as I stare into the rising dark, all I can see are the stars going out, one by one.

"Lucas!"

Ash's muffled shout sounds like it's coming from a million miles away, even though he's sitting right beside me. Glancing back, I see his face contort in fear as he points towards the screen.

"It's coming!"

He's screaming the words straight into my face, but all I hear is a whisper as I turn my gaze towards the screen.

It looks like a jet-black tidal wave, a tsunami of darkness surging towards us without a sound. I watch open-mouthed as the front row of cinema seats is torn out by this onrushing dark, the crimson chairs flipped up into the air before a foaming blackness swallows them whole.

Grabbing hold of my shoulder, Finn yells in my ear but I can't hear a sound. I feel like I'm drowning in silence as the darkness crashes through the cinema.

Directly ahead, I see Caitlin and Maya scrambling out of their seats. Through the gloom I can glimpse the fear in their eyes as they try to outrace the oncoming tide. Catching my gaze, Caitlin starts to scream out a warning but the words never reach me as I see a shadow fall across her face. Maya reaches out towards her with an outstretched arm and for a split-second their frozen figures are silhouetted against the dark. Then the tidal wave sweeps over them and all I can see is blackness.

It's too late to start running, but that's all there's left to do. As the seats flip up behind us, I feel popcorn crunch beneath my feet, the carpet sticky with spilled snacks as I desperately follow in Finn's footsteps. Ash is close behind as we race to the end of the row, the darkness gaining with every step.

Dead ahead, the tidal wave crashes against the wall of the auditorium, its surging current doubling back and smearing Finn out of existence. My heart hammers in my chest, but I can't even hear the sound of my own breathing. With a despairing glance back over my shoulder, I see Ash clambering on top of a cinema seat. Fists clenched, he screams in the face of the onrushing tide and then he's gone. Lost in the maelstrom.

Silence surrounds me – the void swarming in from all sides.

And I feel myself falling into the dark.